Anxie

For my inner anxiety girl.

It's okay to be afraid.

A Note from the Author.

I've always been a worrisome person, but my real struggle with anxiety and depression started around seven years ago. I'm still not a hundred percent sure what exactly triggered my anxiety, but I quickly found myself falling deeper into an anxiety-fuelled depression. I watched the person I was slowly disappear and all that remained was an empty shell of a woman.

Although no two cases of anxiety are the same, I really hope Anxiety Girl can help other sufferers to realise there is a light at the end of the tunnel and that they're not alone in their struggles.

Anxiety and depression can affect people for any period of time and in varying degrees of severity. I wanted to create a story which showed that mental health issues can happen to anyone, regardless of who you are or what you have. I also wanted to address that there aren't any rules with anxiety.

The characters in this novel might be fictitious, but the feelings and emotions experienced are very real.

Lacey London

Anxiety:

A feeling of worry, nervousness or unease about something with an uncertain outcome.

Prologue

Hi! I'm Sadie. Sadie Valentine. You don't know me, but then again, I don't know you. Not yet, anyway, but you will get to know me. You will actually get to know me better than most people on this planet. My aim is for us to become so well acquainted that you will feel comfortable enough to confide all of your fears and feelings in me. That might seem an impossible task right now, however, with a little time and trust we can do exactly that.

It's hard to know a person, isn't it? Like, *really* know them. So many of us have a huge circle of friends, relatives and associates around us, people who we know so very well that we could trust with every breath in our bodies. Unfortunately, there may be times in our lives where we discover our nearest and dearest are not quite as sympathetic as we would like them to be. This isn't because they don't care or that they're not interested, but simply because they don't understand exactly what it is we are going through.

It's easy for us to become frustrated with our families and to get annoyed and upset because we feel like we are alone in our battle with anxiety. The truth is, those closest to us probably feel just as helpless as we do. Not being able to aid a loved one when we can clearly see they're in distress is a torture all of its own. Anxiety, along with other mental health issues, doesn't just affect the sufferer, it spreads its cloud over the people around them. Just like smoking, the second-hand effects pass from one person to another until the smoker finally stubs the cigarette out.

I want you all to know that you are *not* alone. Whether it's anxiety, depression, panic attacks, stress or all four, never feel like you have to face it by yourself. My job is to help you on this journey. To be the person who you can open up to, safe in the knowledge that I know exactly what you are experiencing because I have been through it myself.

Since we can't physically see anxiety, it's often brushed under the carpet. We are so often told it is something that can simply be shrugged off. The reality is, until we address the underlying cause of the anxiety itself, we will never be completely free from it. Anxiety can't be cured with an over-the-counter pill, a quick trip to the doctor's surgery or a browse of the internet for advice and that's a hard thing to accept. Learning to control anxiety takes time, commitment and a desire to change the way we think.

When I was in the throes of anxiety, it seemed so impossibly huge to me. Of course, I had felt *down* before, but this was different. It felt big. Bigger than big. Bigger than any doctor or specialist would ever understand. I was deteriorating. I was literally watching myself fade away. I could feel it nibbling at my thoughts and chomping through my spirit. I knew it was happening, I just couldn't shake it off. Sometimes I could almost see it, sinking its teeth into any glimpse of happiness I might dare to believe in.

I was desperate not to talk about it. The thought of people knowing I had something wrong upstairs was worse than the diagnosis itself. Choosing to ignore it was my way of handling things. If I didn't acknowledge it, I found it easier to believe it wasn't really there.

As I am sure many of you have discovered, mental health is still quite a *taboo* subject. You can have bum implants, a boob job, you can even have a bloody penis enlargement and society won't judge you. But you tell someone you're having a hard time mentally and they want to put you in a white jacket and throw away the key. Okay, so that might be a *slight* exaggeration, but it's true that matters of the mind are frequently ignored. Out of sight, out of mind. Ironically.

Anxiety, along with depression and panic attacks, was the diagnosis I fought so hard against. I refused to believe it. What had I ever done to be part of the unfortunate group who fall victim to this? I'm sure you have all asked yourself that same question. Why me? I muttered those two little words over and over in my mind on a daily basis. What had gone so fundamentally wrong in my brain to cause the bubbly girl people knew and loved to crumble into a sad, lonely and frightened woman?

Thankfully, I am one of the lucky few who managed to beat anxiety and depression before they beat me and now I want to help all of you to do the same. If I didn't have that one person looking out for me, I don't think I would be here today. I would have succumbed to the little voice in the back of my mind that told me to end it once and for all.

In order for you to feel comfortable enough to confide in me, it's only fair that I confide in you first. We all have a story about how we wound up here. Well, this is mine...

Mental health issues affect people the world over, but **you** won't be one of them, will you?

THE CALM BEFORE THE STORM

Chapter 1

'You have the most beautiful eyes I've ever seen.' My new friend growls, his leg trembling uncontrollably as he looks me up and down.

Wrapping my tongue around my straw, I shrug my shoulders and run a hand through my long, blonde hair. His aftershave is musky and overpowering as he leans in close and whispers in my ear. I don't know his name. I would be surprised if he knew mine. What I *do* know is that he has been undressing me with his eyes since the second I walked in here.

Looking around the packed nightclub, I pretend to listen as he brags about his latest business venture. A business venture that I doubt very much exists. Stifling a yawn, I politely smile and lean back in my seat. He thinks that I like him. He thinks that I've been laughing at his rubbish jokes because I just can't get enough. Little does this fool know he's the third so-called millionaire to hit on me this week. He also doesn't know this is all just a game to me. Well, I call it a game, but games are supposed to be fun, aren't they?

Flirting with men in a lame bid to make myself feel better has never been my style, but believe me, I do have my reasons. You see, according to my friend's advice, the best way to get over a man is to get under another one. After almost eight weeks of putting this theory to the test, I am starting to lose hope in this being the way forward for me.

My new playmate drapes an arm around the back of my chair and I make a point of showing him my glass is almost empty. Immediately standing to attention, he jumps to his feet and makes a beeline for the bar. Who knew it was this easy? Watching him leave, I try to find a part of me that is enjoying this charade. Instead of the excitement and adrenaline that I was seeking, I am left feeling emptier than I did before.

Taking the opportunity to top-up my makeup, I slip through the crowds of gyrating people and disappear into the toilets. The music pounds against the walls of the cubicle as I whip out my mirror and gaze at my reflection. Perfect shades of bronze and gold mingle together on my eyelids, making my green eyes look even more piercing than usual. They say the eyes are the window to the soul, but mine seem so distant, so cut off from reality and so closed to the outside world.

Throwing my ridiculously long hair over my shoulder, I use my elbow to unlock the door and hold my wrists beneath the taps. Cold water runs over my pale skin and I find myself wishing it would wash away the tattoo that is imprinted along the inside of my ring finger. My gaze lands on the text and I let out a little laugh. *Forever.* Nothing could be further from the truth. If only I knew back then what I know now.

As it turns out, absolutely *nothing* lasts forever. Everything has to come to an end eventually, whether we like it or not. We're all aware of that deep down, we just don't want to believe it. Instead, we bury our heads in the sand and pretend it won't ever happen, all the while knowing that it will.

Tearing my eyes away from my unfortunate tattoo, I look to my left to see a pretty redhead staring at my hair in awe.

'Your hair is *incredible!*' She gasps, fluffing up her own locks in the mirror and frowning when it falls flat.

'Thank you!' Shooting her a smile, I turn off the tap and shake the excess water from my hands.

'Are you wearing extensions?' Not holding back, she reaches out and grabs a handful of my hair, carefully inspecting each strand.

I shake my head and snatch a paper towel from the machine.

'It's *so* long!' Her jaw drops as she takes a step back and studies me closely. 'What colour do you use on it?'

I get this a lot. Nobody believes me, but my hair is as natural as the day I was born. As a child, I absolutely hated it, but over the years I have grown to love my snow-like mane.

'It's natural.' I offer her a smile and lean towards the mirror to fix my lipstick.

Carefully tracing my cupid's bow, I smack my lips together and remove any smudges with a piece of tissue paper. There's something about wearing red lipstick that makes me feel invincible. It's like a powerful confidence boost that makes women want to be you and men want to sleep with you. Even if you're not feeling that great on the inside, a simple slick of red tells the outside world a different story.

The redhead squints at me suspiciously before letting out a laugh. 'Fine! Don't tell me! Whatever it is, it looks fantastic!'

With a quick wink, she has a final look in the mirror before disappearing into the nightclub. Returning my attention to my reflection, I run my fingers through my hair and spin around to check out my outfit. The black dress floats over my skinny frame, dancing delicately around my thighs. Tugging on the hem, I adjust the spaghetti straps and let out a satisfied sigh.

Despite my daring choice of clothing, I am quite self-conscious about my image. My friends think I do it for attention. They think I grumble about my insecurities because I'm fishing for compliments, but that couldn't be further from the truth. When I look in the mirror, I don't see what other people seem to see in me. I don't see long legs, a flat stomach and a perfectly contoured face. I see a spindly woman who is built like a grasshopper and slightly resembles a horse.

Squeezing past a couple of young girls, I clutch my bag to my chest and throw open the door. It takes a moment for my eyes to adjust to the darkness as I feel my way around the bar. Cutting across the dancefloor, I notice a couple of frosty glasses on the table as I slide into my seat.

'I was beginning to think you had done a runner...' He beams, leaning over and holding the glass to my lips.

Taking it from him, I make sure to brush my fingers against his for a moment longer than necessary and sneak a glance at my watch. I can't keep this up much longer. No matter how hard I try to convince myself that this is helping me on the road back to happiness, I just find the whole routine a bit mundane and dare I say it, extremely boring.

Clinking his glass against mine, he peers at me over the rim and waves around a hotel room key. His bottom lip quivers as he throws back his drink and inches his chair closer to mine. Alright, that's quite enough. Despite Piper's advice, I have absolutely no intention of taking this further than the harmless flirtation that it is.

Glancing over my shoulder, I breathe a sigh of relief as I spot a familiar face hovering by the entrance. It's about bloody time. Pretending to knock my bag onto the floor, I bend down and subtly flash Aldo the signal. Not missing a beat, he gives me a quick nod in response and vanishes into the darkness.

Slowly sliding to the edge of my seat, I rest my chin in my palm and yawn, a sure-fire signal that I am ready to call it a night.

'I've had such a fabulous time tonight.' Reaching out and placing my spare hand on his arm, I give it a little squeeze and drop my phone into my handbag. 'We *must* do it again sometime.' I try my hardest to put some feeling into my voice, but I am pretty sure he can see I'm losing interest.

'You're… you're not going already, are you?' Realising I might be leaving without him seems to sober him up significantly. 'But, the night's still young…'

I give him a coy smile and glance down at the floor, before bringing my eyes up to meet his. 'It's been great to meet you…'

'Julian.' He confirms, not bothered in the slightest that I blatantly haven't bothered to remember his name.

Julian? I swallow a laugh and reach out for the business card that he is eagerly pushing across the table. He couldn't look less like a Julian if he tried.

Stumbling to his feet, he wraps a sweaty arm around my shoulders and gives me that *I want to kiss you* look. Quickly taking a step back, I promise to call him and disappear into the sea of people. I can feel his eyes burning into me as I sashay up the staircase and slip outside. How do people do this for fun? I feel like an actress who has left the stage and can finally drop the strained pretence. Breathing a sigh of relief, I tuck my hair behind my ears and scan the busy street for Aldo.

A sharp whistle grabs my attention and I spin around to see the messy man-bun that I know and love.

'You took your time!' Resting a hand on my bony hip, I narrow my eyes and wait for him to explain himself.

Aldo reaches into the pocket of his leather jacket and pulls out a pack of cigarettes. 'Bella Lake called the salon.' He rolls his eyes and proceeds to light up. 'She needed her hair extensions fixing before the premiere tomorrow.'

'And you didn't think to call?' I automatically link my arm through his as we start to make our way towards the taxi rank.

Aldo shrugs and blows a steady stream of smoke into the air, not bothering to dignify me with a response. His frosty exterior might come across as arrogant, but Aldo is probably my favourite person in the world. Yes, he can be an arsehole and I have come close to throttling him for stealing my Crème de la Mer, but I wouldn't change him. Aldo is my rock, my best friend and my support network, all rolled into one beautiful, homosexual package.

A couple of teenagers outside the pizza place to our right stop talking as we walk past. One of them lets out a wolf whistle before hiding behind her friend, the pair of them giggling manically. With big, blue eyes and an impressive head of hair, Aldo gets more attention from women than most straight men. I look up at him and smile fondly. I can't deny that he's gorgeous, but *annoyingly* gorgeous. You know the kind, those infuriating men who wake-up prettier than any contouring could possibly make happen. The fact that he's an award-winning hairdresser *might* have something to do with Aldo's striking looks. His thick, chocolate waves and baby-lights are the envy of women everywhere.

In the many years that we have been friends, I haven't once let him cut my hair. Whereas everyone else seems to be transfixed by my platinum locks, Aldo has been itching to snip it off since the moment we met. I actually can't remember the last time I stepped inside a hair salon. Over the years, it has inched further and further down my back and now falls neatly at the base of my spine.

'Have you eaten?' Aldo asks, popping my thought bubble with his smoke hoops.

I nod in response and stop to adjust the buckle on my shoe. 'I had tiger prawns and lobster at Il Migliore.'

Aldo rolls his eyes and coughs into the sleeve of his jacket. 'Which fool paid for it this time?'

'His name was *Julian*.' I say Julian with an accent, already knowing that he is going to poke fun.

'Julian...' Aldo repeats slowly, a smirk playing on his lips. 'So, what's that, the second guy this week?'

'Third.' I correct, feeling my cheeks flush violently.

'What's with you lately?' He gives me a sideways glance and bends down to stub out his cigarette. 'You're going through more men than I do conditioning treatments.'

Choosing not to answer, I look down at the ground as light raindrops start to fall from the sky. A cab fires past in the opposite direction and Aldo expertly raises his hand, causing it to do a sudden U-turn in the middle of the road. Holding on to his arm, I step over a puddle and dive into the back of the car.

'Move your arse, Shirley.' Playfully pushing my arm, Aldo jumps in next to me and slams the door.

Shirley isn't my name, but you already know that. What you don't know is the reason that Aldo refuses to call me anything else. I don't tell many people this, but around ten years ago, my mum won the lottery. I don't just mean a few grand, she won the big time. Once the initial shock had worn off, she hired a financial advisor and made some very successful investments. That's how we live here, in Cheshire.

You're probably wondering what my mum's strike of luck has to do with me earning the rather unfortunate nickname of Shirley. Well, when I turned twenty-one, my mother gave me the rather incredible gift of a luxury apartment in the prestigious village of Alderley Edge. A few months after meeting her boyfriend, Mick, she suddenly voiced her concerns that I was getting too dependent and set me up in a home of my own.

I hadn't even put the key in the door when I noticed the ill-fated spelling mistake on my letter box. Shirley. Shirley Valentine. That movie haunted me throughout my teenage years and now it is going to stick with me until the day I die. I still don't know whether it was an unfortunate error or a lame joke on behalf of the estate agent. Either way, it's going nowhere. The only person to ever see the hapless mistake was my new neighbour. The neighbour who eventually turned out to be my best friend.

Whilst we are on the subject of aliases, Aldo isn't Aldo's real name either. Believe it or not, he was born a not-so-exotic Alan. Yes, the Italian stallion was once Alan Christopher Taylor. In all fairness, Alan is probably the *last* name I would choose for him. Apparently, introducing himself as Aldo led to him getting more action at the local gay bars and after years of juggling the two names, he finally bit the bullet and legally became Aldo Cristiano Taylor.

These days Aldo and I share an apartment. It turns out that being a hairdresser to the stars doesn't pay as well as you might think. Well, not when you spend your entire month's wages on champagne and tattoos. I look over at Aldo and run my eyes over the many inkings on his neck. It's actually his fault that I ended up with the black squiggle on my finger.

With him being literally covered in sketches, he thought the only suitable gift for my twenty-fifth would be a doodle of my own. Little did we know at the time that the tattoo in question would be the start of my demise. I say demise, but that's probably a little strong for what really happened, although at the time it felt exactly that.

An awful churning sensation hits my stomach as I recall my last birthday. The day where everything changed...

Chapter 2

His name was Spencer. Spencer Carter. I knew from the moment I saw him that I wanted him and not just for one night, I wanted him forever. Just like in the movies, our eyes met across a smoky room. There was no wine or cheap perfume, but still, it was a feeling I shall remember forever. When I think back to the fateful day that he came into my life, I never would have believed it would end in such heartache.

It all started on a minibreak to Brighton with a group of girlfriends. We arrived on the Thursday evening and within two hours of being there, our paths had already crossed multiple times. Everywhere I looked he was there, smiling at me from behind his bottle of Corona. It was like it was meant to be. Destiny. Or at least, that's what I told myself. I just knew that he felt the same as I did. No one had ever looked at me that way before. I can still remember how his eyes seemed to look deep into my soul and I was powerless to stop it. It was like the world stopped spinning and everything around me fell into silence.

He toyed with me all evening. Like a spider, he cast his web and just waited for me to make a foul move so that he could pounce. I must have walked past ten times in a desperate bid for him to strike up a conversation with me. Despite my efforts, it was just before midnight that we finally exchanged more than lustful glances. I *accidentally* spilt my drink down his shirt and he *accidentally* brushed my breasts whilst helping me clear it up.

A sad smile plays on the corner of my lips as the taxi takes a sharp left turn. We were so happy. Blissfully happy. Before Spencer, I never believed in love. Not real love, anyway. The kind of love you see in movies where you just can't breathe without one another seemed false to me somehow. Spencer changed more than my outlook on life, he changed me in ways that I never believed possible.

For months we didn't spend a single night apart. If he wasn't up in Cheshire, I was on a train down to Brighton. We spent day after day wrapped up in one another, both physically and emotionally. We talked about everything. From books and ice-cream, to children and plans for the future. Within days he knew more about me than anyone else ever had. He completed me. He made me into the person that I always wanted to be. Strong, confident and trusting. I guess it was the last one that got me into trouble.

When I close my eyes, I can still see his face as though he is stood right in front of me. The little scar above his left eyebrow. The random streak of grey in his dark, floppy hair. The extraordinarily white teeth that at first, I was convinced were fake. The way the skin wrinkled around his eyes when his face broke into a smile. Spencer had one of those smiles that could light up an entire room. Just like his smile, his personality was larger than life. Everywhere he went, people wanted a piece of him. It was like he had a secret, a secret that other people just *had* to find out.

In true whirlwind style, we were engaged in a matter of months. He didn't have a ring, but that didn't matter to me at all. My friends couldn't comprehend that part, but our relationship went deeper than materialistic things. We understood one another on a much higher level and didn't expect the rest of society to recognize that. We didn't need them to. It was us against the world and we reminded ourselves of that every single day.

I look out of the window and watch the streets whizz by as I think back to the day where I felt everything had finally fallen into place. Spencer woke me up at the crack of dawn. It was the height of summer, so daylight was already streaming in through the open windows. Without saying a word, he tossed me some clothes and planted a soft kiss on my cheek. Totally intrigued, I dragged on my denim shorts and followed him out to the car. Despite my incessant probing, Spencer didn't give me more than a mysterious smile for the entire journey, which only fuelled my fire.

When we finally came to a stop, the sun was high in the sky, casting a blinding, white light over us. I laughed and giggled like a teenager as he took my hand in his and led me across the hot sand. The beach was secluded. The only signs of life came in the form of a few random seagulls that scoured the area for food. With the sea breeze blowing through my hair and warmth from the sun enveloping my body, I had never felt more free.

Spencer's oversized t-shirt billowed in the wind as he strode across the sand. His long fingers entwined with mine, he calmly guided me to the perfect spot. My heart raced when we stopped where the ocean kisses the shore. Taking my face in his hands, he kissed me deeply on the lips before dropping to his knees. My ears started to ring as I registered what was happening. I didn't believe it. I didn't dare to in case that tiny shred of doubt in my mind was right. Then he said it.

Will you marry me?

I didn't say a word. I didn't need to. He knew without even asking that I would say *yes*. My entire body prickled with adrenaline as he pulled me down onto the sand. The sun danced on the water, creating a dazzling congratulatory display. We must have stayed in that same spot for hours, completely lost in one another's embrace. I never wanted to get up. I never wanted to return to the real world for fear that it would take away the sentiment of our special day.

The cab comes to a sudden stop and I am jolted back to reality with a bump. Shaking all thoughts of Spencer out of my head, I reach into my bag and pass the driver some coins. Aldo's phone rings loudly as he steps out of the cab and I can't help but notice him smile as he presses the handset to his ear. Sliding over the cold seat, I adjust my dress before pushing myself to my feet. Aldo marches on ahead and I follow behind, taking extra care not to step in any puddles in my very expensive shoes.

Our building is quite something to look at, although the magic of the place doesn't have the same effect on you after many years of calling it home. Situated on a leafy lane, the apartment block is set back from the road, safely hidden behind a set of tall, iron gates. Due to its secluded location, you don't really see many people milling about. Well, apart from the photographers who are desperately seeking a shot of the latest United signing. The white frontage is kept pristine by the many cleaners and maintenance guys who work so hard at making sure not a single leaf is out of place. The glass doors that lead you inside give the impression of a high-end, boutique hotel. Minimalistic, sleek and luxurious.

Aldo jabs at the lift button with a black fingernail and the doors immediately swing open. Quickening my pace, I step inside and sneak a peek at Aldo's phone.

'Who was that?' I ask casually, already knowing the answer. 'Edward?'

Aldo purses his lips and I roll my eyes in response. Edward is Aldo's latest squeeze and just like the rest of his futile relationships, I expect this one to fizzle out any day now. Unlike Aldo, Edward is as extroverted as can be. With a peroxide quiff, acrylic nail extensions and a mahogany tan, he is most definitely Aldo's polar-opposite.

'Is he coming over?' I ask, as the lift comes to a stop and we step out onto our floor.

Aldo yawns and shakes his head. 'No, he's travelling to London. He's got a modelling shoot in the morning...'

'Does that mean he's having an early night?'

'It means he's drinking tequila shots from the photographer's crotch and wants me to join him.' Taking a set of keys out of his back pocket, he fiddles with the lock and lets us into the apartment.

I let out a giggle, knowing that Aldo's Friday nights usually involve this kind of thing anyway.

Following him inside, I immediately kick off my shoes and wander over to the balcony. It might be damp and wet outside, but the air is thick and humid. Throwing open the doors, I take a deep breath and look out over the expansive woodland below. The last of the leaves rustle in the breeze, creating a calming soundtrack to the eerie silence of the forest. A lot of people would find this darkness unnerving, but it makes me feel free. I don't quite know why, it just does.

The bareness, the nothingness. It's like a blank canvas, just waiting for someone to pick up a pen and colour it in.

Tearing myself away, I throw myself onto one of the plush loungers and stretch out my legs, just as Aldo appears with two glasses of fizz. Placing them on the table, he feels around in his pocket before producing an electronic cigarette. Attempting to take a drag, he shakes it vigorously and frowns before tossing it onto the floor in anger.

'Damn thing...' Cursing under his breath, he disappears inside and returns with a packet of Marlboro Lights.

'Aldo...' I mutter disapprovingly, watching him light up and inhale deeply.

Shaking my head, I look up at the black sky and take in the blanket of stars. The more I look, the more seem to appear. I trace my eyes from one sparkle to the next, completely transfixed by their presence.

Reaching out for the glass of bubbles, my fingers don't reach the stem when I hear a ping from inside the apartment. Begrudgingly rolling off my lounger, I head off in search of my phone. Quickly discovering it on the kitchen island, I use the control panel on the wall to put on some gentle music. Tossing my hair over my shoulder, I wander outside and tap at the handset with my finger. An email pops up on the screen and I feel my heart pound as I take in the text.

'Yes!' I exclaim, fist pumping the air happily. 'Finally!'

Aldo looks at me curiously as I do a little victory dance around the balcony.

'Precious have sold *three* of my paintings!' I squint at the email, double checking the number of zeros.

Nodding in approval, he drains the contents of his glass and smiles. 'It's about time, isn't it? It's been months since you last sold anything...'

'I know!' I shout over my shoulder, dashing to the champagne fridge for more bubbles. 'I was beginning to question my creative flair...'

'Creative flair!' Aldo scoffs, throwing back his head and laughing. 'Please! You know what they say about fools and their money...'

Popping the cork on the chilled bottle, I turn my back to the wind to stop my hair from sticking to my lip-gloss. 'And this is coming from the man who charges two hundred quid for a cut and blow-dry?'

'Touché...' He lets out a laugh and holds up his glass for a refill.

In case you are wondering, Precious is a bar in a neighbouring village that displays my artwork to its customers. Frequented by the glitterati, it is easy to scoop four figures for a painting. Not long ago I was selling ten pieces a week, giving me more money than I really knew what to do with, but things have changed quite a bit over the past twelve months. I can't remember the last time I received a cheque from Precious and between you and me, I was getting a little worried.

It's true that I own the apartment outright, but running a place like this doesn't come cheap. In fact, it's downright extortionate. I know what you're thinking. Poor little rich girl being made to stand up to the plate and pay her way, but I did find it tough. When you haven't had much guidance in your life, it's scary to try and fend for yourself for the first time. I've never had a good relationship with my mum, but when she handed over the keys to this place things went from bad to worse. It's almost as though the apartment was given in exchange for abandoning her role as a mother. Don't get me wrong, we exchange the odd text message and go for a coffee once in a while, but close we most certainly are not.

To be completely honest, a lot of it is down to her boyfriend, Mick. Despite my efforts to make him like me, we never got along. He believed that I was spoilt. I can still hear him now.

You're ruining her, Linda. You're creating a monster. If you don't put a stop to this now, she will still be living here when she's fifty.

Kind of rich coming from the man who spends my mum's money like it's going out of fashion. They were only together for six months before she bought him a Range Rover. I laugh silently and take a sip of my drink. My mum swears it's not about the money, but it's hard to agree when you see him flying around Wilmslow with his mates in the back of her Bentley. For a guy who prided himself on being a beer-swilling man of the people, he soon got comfortable with the champagne lifestyle.

I look down into my glass and watch the bubbles race to the top, each one disappearing with a pop as they hit the surface. Just like my relationship with my mother, slowly fizzing away one bubble at a time.

My eyes start to feel heavy as Aldo clears his throat, catching my attention.

'Cheers, Shirley.' Raising his glass in the air, he clinks it against mine and winks. 'Congrats on your sale.'

Replying with a smile, I take a gulp and allow my eyes to close. Money doesn't buy happiness, I can testify to that, but it does provide stability and at this point in my life, stability is exactly what I need.

Chapter 3

Studying the canvas in front of me, I screw up my nose as I take in my latest piece. Splashes of black and grey fill the once white space, creating a complicated blur of metallic smears. My eyes trace the strokes of my brush as I try to envisage the final effect. Deciding that a dash of scarlet wouldn't hurt, I scour my pots for the correct shade and coat the tip of my brush. I promised myself this canvas wouldn't be monochrome like the rest of my work, but no matter how hard I try to use the brighter end of the palette, I just can't seem to work with those colours. It's like they don't speak to me in the same way that dark tones do.

My friends joke I would sell more pieces if they weren't as solemn and gloomy, so I've been making a conscious effort to play around with colour more. Flicking my brush across the fabric, I grimace as splashes of red land amongst the black, instantly regretting it.

When I first moved here, I found it quite difficult to make friends. Not drinking buddies, I had more of those than I could keep track of, but actual relationships were hard to find. As a self-confessed tomboy, I had more fun filling a backpack and losing myself in the local woodland. Breaking a sweat whilst exploring the many nature trails gives me more of a high than any bar or club ever could, but trying to find a mate who had the same interests proved tricky, to say the least. I soon discovered that most girls my age were more interested in bagging the next footballer or millionaire playboy.

After a year or so of struggling to fit in, I eventually gave up on the idea of having a hiking pal and kept my forest adventures a secret. My, *if you can't beat them, join them* attitude soon resulted in me gaining a few additions to my phonebook. Aldo aside, Piper, Ivy and Zara have become my closest allies and the four of us are often seen together in Cheshire's celebrity haunts. It was actually Piper who encouraged me to dive back into the dating game, although I must admit it doesn't come as easily to me as it does to her.

Born to the richest power couple in the village, Piper used her blessed upbringing to start a life coaching business. Teaching others how to recreate her lifestyle for themselves has resulted in her gaining a reputation in the Cheshire triangle as a mastermind guru. It's unbelievable what people will pay for tips on how to obtain a rich husband and the latest sports car.

At just five feet tall, Piper really is a storm in a teacup. Her larger than life, high-maintenance personality is a little shocking considering her petite appearance. With golden skin, tumbling black locks and a pout fuller than Irina Shayk, she is everything you would imagine a Cheshire princess to be. Don't be fooled though, her butter wouldn't melt exterior is not a reflection of what lies beneath.

Piper is famed in the village for not pulling any punches and saying exactly what is on her mind, even if she knows it's going to hurt someone's feelings. Some would describe her as ruthless, but she prefers honest and real. Even after a few years of friendship, I'm still not sure what side of the fence I sit on.

Thankfully, Ivy and Zara aren't quite so scary, although they're just as beautiful. Twin sisters of an American couple from London, Ivy and Zara made the move up to Cheshire after appearing on a reality TV show. Said TV show led to Ivy having a short-term relationship with a member of the City football team. A few months later, Zara followed suit in search of a sports star of her own. Much to Ivy's dismay, her footballer beau soon decided that he hadn't had enough of the single life and ended their whirlwind relationship no sooner than it began. These days, the three of them put all their efforts into trying to catch the eye of a millionaire, or in Piper's case, a billionaire.

Attempting to scratch my nose with paint-covered fingers, I curse under my breath as a blob of grey lands on my dungarees. I know an artist painting in dungarees is such a terrible cliché, but it has become my uniform. My denim dungarees and faded Oasis t-shirt are the two things I just can't seem to work without.

Abandoning my brush, I tiptoe across the cold tiles and into the kitchen. With Aldo at work, I have the whole apartment to myself, which is something I am still a little uneasy with. Sometimes I crave solitude, but once I am alone with my thoughts, I get this sense of nervousness that makes me uncomfortable. It's like I need to know there's someone else other than me in the vicinity. Not necessarily to talk to, just knowing that they are there is enough.

The sun peeps out from behind the layer of grey cloud, shining a bright light into the apartment. Stepping towards the windows,

I close my eyes and enjoy the blissful sensation of warmth on my skin. If I didn't know any better, I would swear I was on a beach somewhere. As much as I love Alderley Edge, I would give anything to live by the ocean. I've always loved to be in water, it's where I feel the most at peace with myself. I blame it on my star sign, Pisces. Some people don't believe in astrology, but with me, it is right on the money.

Before I can stop it, my brain flits to the last time I was at the seaside and my heart pangs with longing. It has been two months since my breakup with Spencer and even though I've been bleeding inside ever since, I've never once allowed the pain to spill out. A part of me believes that if I can hold it together until the memory fades, then it never really happened. I don't just mean the breakup. I mean all of it. Brighton, the broken promises and the meaningless engagement. Not allowing myself to cry about things has made me question if it is fiction or reality. As time passes, I genuinely struggle to separate what actually happened from the film reel I've built up in my mind.

Piper thought Spencer was a horrendous idea from the second she laid eyes on him. Once she discovered he wasn't set to inherit a fortune and didn't have some genius invention up his sleeve that was about to earn him a million, she wrote him off immediately. Her attitude towards Spencer has made it a little easier to get over him. The absence of the dreaded breakup questions regarding how I am coping has enabled me to keep a stiff upper lip.

Ivy and Zara have been a little more sympathetic, but even they couldn't fathom how I could be so consumed by someone that I had known for such a short space of time. I don't expect them to understand as I still don't understand it myself. What was it about him that made me forget reality existed? How did he make me believe in fairy tales and happily ever after? He was just a guy like any other. Two arms, two legs and one heart. Looking back, I find it hard to accept that Spencer had a heart. If he did he wouldn't have treated me so cruelly.

Almost unbelievably, Aldo loved Spencer as much as I did. From the second they were introduced they became the best of friends. Unlike the girls, Aldo believed that Spencer and I were destined to be together, which meant a lot when you consider he doesn't believe in soulmates. He won't admit it, but I know the breakup hurt him almost as much as it hurt me. Regardless of what kind of relationship you have with a person, when trust is broken it's a pain that just can't be explained.

Dragging myself away from the window, I exhale loudly and wander across the open living area. Sometimes I wonder if Aldo and I really need a place so big. I often consider downsizing and pocketing the cash, but the view from up here is so spectacular that I don't think I could ever leave it. You're probably thinking that keeping an apartment solely for the view is a little silly, but that view has pulled me through some pretty tough times in the past. It's like no matter what's going on in my life, the trees are always there, standing proud and tall as they wrap their protective arms around the building.

Suddenly remembering I sold some pieces yesterday, I dig out my mobile to text my mum. As my fingers tap the keyboard, I find myself wondering why I bother striving for her approval. She has made it quite clear over the years that she thinks my career is a joke. She hasn't ever used that word, but she certainly doesn't hold back when sharing her thoughts on my choice of occupation. I try not to take it to heart, but it still hurts when your own mother disapproves of the one thing you're passionate about.

Deciding to contact her anyway, I let out a sigh and hit *send.* Selling a few paintings isn't going to fix our relationship, but one thing I've learned is that you only fail when you stop trying...

Chapter 4

Pulling up outside Precious, I swing my car into the last remaining space and turn off the engine. As usual, the road is starting to fill up with clusters of photographers, each one snapping away at the fleet of super-cars across the street. Not giving them a second glance, I throw open the door and make my way inside.

Nestled between a prestigious wine bar and a fabulous Greek restaurant, Precious is the bar of choice for Cheshire's social butterflies. With its glamorous, rococo interior, it really is the best place to showcase my work. The imposing chandelier hangs beautifully in the centre of the room, flooding the dark bar with light. Scanning the area, I take a seat at one of the plush booths and look around for the manager. In true Patrick style, the music is already playing and the tables are dressed for service, despite the fact they don't open for another couple of hours.

Hearing footsteps behind me, I spin around in my seat to see Patrick striding out of the kitchen.

'Sadie! What a fabulous outfit!' Holding out his arms, he envelopes me in a bear hug. 'So... *arty!*' Smoothing down his black shirt, he sits down opposite me. 'And I just *love* the paint splatter. Great touch!'

I've always liked Patrick. Always smiling, always immaculately dressed and always the perfect gentleman. Taking a cheque from his shirt pocket, he places it face down on the table and runs over to the bar. I watch him use various bottles to create two elaborate cocktails and give him a quick round of applause.

'Alcohol-free, before you protest.' Patrick grins and clinks his glass against mine.

Eyeing up the vivid concoction, I take a sip and nod in approval. 'Very nice. What's the occasion?'

Patrick's smile falters for a moment as he looks down at the cheque and slides it across the table.

'I don't quite know how to say this...' His cheeks flush violently and I shoot him a questioning glance. 'Kieran and I have been talking and I'm afraid we can't display your work here anymore.'

I pause with my lips clamped around the straw and frown. 'I'm sorry?' I mumble, thinking that I've misheard him.

He bites his lip and frowns apologetically. 'Kieran thinks it *lowers the tone* of the premises.'

My jaw drops open and I stare at him in shock. 'Lowers the tone?' I repeat, suddenly feeling a little sick. 'Since when?'

Patrick looks so flustered that I actually feel sorry for him. 'We hired an interior designer and they came up with a whole bunch of new ideas. Removing the artwork was the first thing on their list.' Patrick reaches over and places a sympathetic hand on my arm. 'This isn't personal. I do hope you understand.'

Trying to regain the use of my tongue, I lick my lips and nod slowly. 'It's fine. You have to do what's best for your business.'

I attempt a small smile, but inside I feel completely thrown. Even though I've been going through a dry patch lately, I had a good thing going here.

'I really hope this isn't going to affect our friendship?' Patrick looks at me nervously and squirms in his seat.

'No, of course not!' I take another sip of my cocktail and try to keep my voice light. 'Don't be silly.'

'Thank God!' Patrick breathes a sigh of relief and laughs dramatically. 'I was so worried about having this conversation with you. I haven't slept a wink all night!'

I let out a tiny laugh and shake my head. It's not the end of the world, is it? In business, you have to make decisions that are going to upset other people, but if you can't stand the heat, get out of the kitchen.

'It's fine, Patrick. Honestly, I completely understand.' I stir my straw around the glass and try to think of it practically. 'I guess I should head home and call around some other venues...'

'No need!' He reaches into his pocket and holds up a list of phone numbers. 'I felt so bad about the whole situation, so I pulled a few strings and these have all agreed to talk with you.'

Feeling genuinely touched by his act of kindness, I lean across the table and take the note from him. 'You didn't have to do that, Patrick. Thank you so much.'

'It was the least I could do.' He waves off my gratitude and motions to the bar. 'Now, can I get you another drink?'

Shaking my head in response, I push away my glass and slide off my seat. 'I better get going. Thank you, Patrick and I don't just mean for the cheque. You've been really good to me over the past few years. I won't forget it.'

Patrick's bottom lip trembles ever so slightly and he throws his arms around my neck. Squeezing tightly, he plants a kiss on my forehead and points to the paintings on the wall. 'You get yourself home. I'll run the remaining pieces over to your place whenever you're ready.'

Thanking him once again, I grab my car keys and head for the door. The sun shines in my eyes as a fleet of teenage girls run past, waving their cameras in the air excitedly. Their high-pitched squeals are contagious as they race along the road, leaving a cloud of perfume in their wake. When I first moved into the village, bumping into celebrities gave me such a buzz, but just like anything else, it becomes the norm after a while.

Beeping open the car, I fire up the engine and pull out onto the open road. The cosmopolitan lane is lined with more bars, restaurants and boutique shops than you could ever imagine. I don't think I will ever tire of this place. Whether you want to kick back with a coffee or join the socialites with a glass of bubbles, Alderley Edge has something for everyone. With the paparazzi on every corner, I sometimes forget that I'm in such a rural location, but as soon as I leave the main strip and enter the rolling, country roads there's no denying where I am.

Brown leaves fall onto the windscreen as I speed along the road. Craning my neck, I look up at the trees overhead as they entwine their branches together in a warm embrace. Despite the unfortunate situation with Precious, I feel surprisingly positive. Maybe I will strike an amazing deal with one of these other venues and look back on this as the best thing that ever happened to me. Twisting from left to right, I find myself dreaming about selling hundreds of pieces and finally making my mother proud of me.

I've lost count of the number of times she's given me that look. You know the one. The look that says, *I'm constantly disappointed in you, but I'm tired of saying it. I'm just going to stare at you with a saddened look in my eye and hope that you get the message.* My heart sinks as I realise that I have to tell her about Patrick dropping my work. She will only find out from someone else and give me an even harder time about it. This is a small village and people talk.

Deciding to call through Patrick's list the minute I get home, I flick on the radio and stare at the road ahead. My eyes trace the curvature of the lane as I follow the familiar route that has become so dear to me. Even after all these years, I still can't believe that I live here. I, Sadie Valentine, girl from the estate, now lives in the eye-wateringly expensive Golden Triangle. With footballers for neighbours and champagne chilling in my fridge, you would think I'd been born into this privileged lifestyle, but that couldn't be further from the truth.

You see, my mum was just a teenager when she fell pregnant with me. The only daughter of an alcoholic father and a sick mother, she wasn't exactly given the best start in life. Her first encounter with a boy left her sixteen and pregnant. My heart pangs when I think of just how hard it must have been for her. Fleeing her family home, she chose to live with her cousin and raise me alone when the boy inevitably disappeared from the scene.

Needless to say, I've never known my biological father and the many boyfriends my mum acquired over the years showed little interest in me. Until recently, I didn't put much thought into who my real dad is, but when Spencer proposed, I developed this overwhelming urge to discover who I really was. I realise that putting a face to the name won't change who I am as a person, but something inside has a craving to know whose genes I am made up of.

My mother has always been completely against the idea. The first and last time I asked about him, she burst into tears and threw a piece of paper at me with a name hastily scribbled in the corner. That same piece of paper resides in my purse today.

Neatly folded between the many bank cards and my driving license, I haven't dared to look at it in years. I can still picture her face, screwed up with disgust as she launched it at me in a fit of rage. *Don't you dare come crying to me when he breaks your heart like he did mine.* Secretly, I always thought she was incredibly dramatic over the situation. They were just a couple of kids who didn't understand what they were getting themselves into.

Despite her insistence that he isn't worth knowing, I can't help but think she's wrong. Time changes people. *People* change people. For all we know, he has regretted walking away every single day of his life. Maybe he's spent the last twenty-five years wondering about the little girl he left behind. I've never told anyone this before, but I have this secret fantasy that he knows who I am and has been watching me from afar. Almost like a guardian angel. The idea of him looking out for me is a lot easier to swallow than thinking he hasn't ever given me a second thought.

Coming to a stop at my building, I pull on the handbrake and wait for the gates to open. Feeling a tear slip down my cheek, I furiously bat it away and fix my face in the rear-view mirror, all thoughts of what and

who I am concealed behind a strained
smile.

Chapter 5

'Just answer it...' Picking up his bottle of Evian, Aldo grabs his cigarettes and heads for the balcony. 'What's the worst that can happen?'

Looking down at the vibrating handset, I feel my stomach flip. When I arrived home earlier, I poured myself a coffee and settled down to find a new venue to host my work. My optimistic attitude soon deteriorated when I crossed the last name off Patrick's list. It turns out that I had a *great* deal with Patrick. Not only did Precious advertise my pieces for free, they only took a measly ten percent from the sale price. The only other establishment who showed an interest demanded at least half of the profits.

Aldo has spent the last hour attempting to convince me that something will come up, but inside I feel devastated. An ear-bashing from my mum is the last thing I need right now. Feeling totally dejected, I take a deep breath and jab at the screen until it springs to life.

'Hi, Mum.' Stretching out on the couch, I brace myself for what I am about to hear.

'*Hi, Mum?*' She repeats sarcastically, the sound of her voice immediately grating on me. 'You always sound so bloody miserable, Sadie!'

Choosing to ignore her, I run my thumb over my finger tattoo. 'How are you?'

'She's great!' Mick's voice comes down the line, making my skin itch with repulsion.

'Am I on speakerphone?' I ask, scowling in annoyance. 'Why am I on speakerphone?'

'I'm painting my nails!' She trills, laughing as Mick starts to sing in the background. 'Anyway, I just called to let you know that we're going away for a while...'

'You've only just come back from Thailand.' My nose screws up as I recall the many sozzled photos from Bangkok. 'Where are you going this time?'

'I don't think that's any of your business, Sadie!' Mick shouts, clearly intoxicated. 'Where and when we choose to go on holiday is nothing to do with...'

'*Mick!*' My mum hisses, her voice muffled as she covers the receiver. 'Just ignore him. We're going to Dubai for a month. The weather's starting to turn and we don't want to be around to see the trees go bare.'

'You don't need to justify it to me. Like Mick said, it's none of my business...' I smile at Aldo as he steps back inside the apartment.

She laughs and attempts to conceal the awkwardness with a cough. 'Anyway, where have you been hiding? I can't remember the last time I saw you!'

The fact my mother and I haven't bothered to pay one another a visit in almost eight weeks when we live just a ten-minute drive apart speaks volumes about the state of our relationship.

'I've been busy.' I lie, ignoring the churning sensation in my stomach. 'I was going to call you later. Precious can't display my pieces anymore...'

She inhales sharply and I close my eyes, instantly regretting my decision to tell her.

'Why?' The immediate accusatory tone to her voice is all too familiar. 'What have you done?'

'I haven't done anything. They are having a revamp and selling art isn't going to fit in with their new image...'

'Yeah, right!' Mick cackles loudly. 'So, what's next? Are you finally going to grow up and get a real job?'

I open my mouth to respond, but change my mind at the last moment. I know better than to try and argue with Mick when he's had a drink.

'He does have a point.' My mum says decidedly. 'You're twenty-five now, Sadie. Isn't it about time that you stopped messing around with these... *paintings?* You've got a bloody degree! Why don't you use it?'

Not bothering to reply, I slide across the couch to make room for Aldo.

'You need to sort yourself out. Don't be thinking that *I'm* going to bail you out. I've been more than good enough to you. This is a wake-up call. It's time for you to grow up.'

Resisting the urge to remind her that I haven't asked for a penny since she handed over the keys to this place, I let out a yawn and drape my legs across Aldo's lap. Any other mother would be incredibly proud of their daughter being an artist, but not my mum. I learned years ago that nothing I ever do will be good enough for her. I cast my mind back to the days before Mick and try to remember if things were always this way. The truth is, she was never around long enough to be disappointed in me.

'Anyway, I don't want to talk about this right now.' She sighs dramatically and whispers something to Mick. 'We're going to be away from Wednesday. Try and get yourself sorted by the time we're back.'

After reluctantly agreeing to check on her house, I let out a silent scream and toss the handset onto an adjacent chair. Surely it's not normal to feel like you've been given a blow to the stomach after speaking to your mother? To feel so dejected and low after hearing her voice?

'Well?' Aldo asks, taking a sip of water.

'Don't ask.' Shaking my head in response, I roll onto my side and snuggle into the cushions. 'Same old, same old...'

I twist my hair into a messy bun and try my best to ignore the sorrowful look on Aldo's face. He's never been able to understand the strained bond I have with my mother. With him having such a fabulous connection with his own parents, he can't comprehend the dysfunctional dynamic of our relationship.

'I'm sorry...' Aldo sighs, draping an arm around my shoulder.

'Don't be sorry!' I force myself to smile and bat him away, mortified that he's pitying me. 'She's always been this way. It's nothing new to me.'

'Doesn't it bother you?' Fiddling with his watch, he stares at me intently. 'Don't you wish she was a *little* more supportive?'

Not wanting to say how I really feel, I try my hardest not to look bothered. 'Like I said, she's always been the same.'

Parents are supposed to give you a helping hand when you're rock bottom, not kick you when you're already down. I think back to the day that Spencer broke things off. I felt like my heart had been ripped out of my throat and smashed into a million pieces, yet all she said was, *there's plenty more fish in the sea*. I remember my body physically aching from the shock of her dismissal. The sadness, the grief and the dismay sent me into a state of shock. I still don't know how I managed to sit there and smile at her collection of holiday photos as though nothing had happened. As though my entire life, my entire future hadn't just been snatched away from me.

'Do you want to go out for a while?' Aldo asks suddenly, piercing my thought bubble. 'It's still early, we could grab dinner and a few drinks?'

I glance down at my watch and shrug my shoulders. 'If I say *yes* will you do my hair?'

Grabbing my ponytail, I wave it in his face and giggle as his eyes widen in horror at the state of my split ends.

Letting out a scoff, he shoves my legs to the floor and heads towards his bedroom. 'Only if you let me cut it off...'

Chapter 6

Flashing his black card at the doorman, Aldo reaches for my hand as we make our way inside the bar. With it being a weekday, the place is reasonably quiet and it doesn't take us long to spot Ivy and Zara at their favourite table. Wearing their trademark skinny jeans and fitted blazers, they shake their caramel hair extensions as they pose for selfies. Weaving our way through the smattering of people, I raise my hand in acknowledgment as Ivy waves her glass in the air.

'Do we *have* to sit with them?' Aldo moans, checking out his perfect man-bun in the mirror and smoothing down a stray hair.

'Don't be like that.' Giving his arm a squeeze, I lower my voice to a whisper. 'Just one drink and then we can go somewhere else.'

Not looking in the least bit pacified, he replies with a scowl as we come to a stop at their table. 'Fine, but if Piper shows up, I'm leaving.'

It's no secret that Aldo and Piper don't see eye-to-eye. I've lost count of the number of times I have had to play referee to stop them from tearing each other's hair out.

'Look what the cat dragged in...' Zara teases, taking a sip of her pink bubbles as she shoots Aldo a wink.

Not sticking around to respond, Aldo shakes off his leather jacket and hops onto a stool at the bar.

'What's with him?' Ivy asks, her plump pout even larger than normal. 'That time of the month?'

Zara lets out a snigger and I can't help but notice a nose ring where her diamond stud normally resides. Choosing to ignore her, I pull out a chair as Ivy adds another layer of gloss to her lips.

'So, I heard about Precious...' Zara whispers, nudging Ivy as she speaks.

'Wow, good news travels fast.' I manage, struggling to keep a poker face.

'What are you going to do?' Clearly not sensing my tone, Zara continues to push the subject. 'You're technically jobless now, right?'

I look up as Aldo places a couple of glasses down on the table. 'I don't think

Shirley wants to talk about it.' He raises a perfect eyebrow at her and takes his seat. 'Besides, you two haven't worked a day in your lives, you're not exactly In a position to be dishing out career advice.'

'Who's rattled your cage?' Ivy scoffs, immediately jumping to her sister's defence.

'Get your roots done.' Aldo fires back, not missing a beat.

Hiding a smile behind my glass, I resist the urge to let out a giggle. Every single time they're together it's the same. The twins rile up Aldo and he snaps back. Neither side wanting to be the first to give in, this charade usually continues until Piper makes an appearance and Aldo storms off.

'Piper should be here shortly.' Zara muses, as though reading my mind. 'She's having dinner with Robert Henshaw....'

'Robert Henshaw!' Aldo repeats, almost choking on his drink. 'Isn't he about eighty?'

Ivy and Zara laugh simultaneously and shake their heads.

'He's not *eighty!*' Zara retorts, digging out a compact mirror to check her makeup. 'He's sixty-five!'

Staring at her incredulously, Aldo curls up his lip and frowns. As I mentioned earlier, my friend's insistence on finding themselves rich husbands really grinds Aldo's gears. Giving him a nudge under the table, I watch a waitress carry two plates of steaming food through the bar. Despite Aldo's offer of dinner earlier, he tossed me a packet of crisps as we left the apartment and promised to grab a takeout on the way home.

Ignoring my rumbling stomach, I disguise a yawn with a cough and pretend to listen as Ivy and Zara fill me in on their week. I am nodding along aimlessly when a certain name catches my attention.

'He sent Ivy a Friend Request on Facebook...' Zara whispers, studying me closely for a reaction.

I feel the blood drain from my face and frantically try to hide it. Not knowing what to say, I look up at Aldo for help.

'I mean, what would *Spencer* want to connect with Ivy for?' She screws up her tiny nose and I can't help noticing the slight smile that is playing on her lips.

'Zara!' Ivy hisses, giving her a discreet nudge. 'I told you not to say anything!' Turning her attention to me, she forces herself to smile and blushes. 'Don't worry, I ignored it.'

Feeling my skin prickle with shock, I purse my lips and nod in response. As much as I am trying to act nonchalant, this little snippet of information has really bothered me. From the day that Spencer told me it was over, I haven't heard a peep from him. Not an apologetic text, not a drunken phone call, nothing.

'Are *you* still friends with Spencer on Facebook?' Zara asks Aldo, leaning over the table and raising an eyebrow mischievously. 'You two got along so well...'

Obviously sensing that Spencer isn't something I want to talk about, Aldo scowls at Zara and slams his drink down on the table. 'What is it with you two tonight? You're like the Witches of Eastwick!'

'I'm just curious!' Zara protests, frowning and sitting back in her seat. 'Sadie hasn't breathed his name since they split, now that he's back on the scene it's only natural to ask a couple of questions!'

'Maybe that's Shirley's way of dealing with things.' Aldo growls, not backing down. 'We don't all shag everything that moves when we've had our hearts broken...'

'From what I hear, she's been doing that too...' Ivy giggles and sways around to the music.

Completely mortified, I look around the room for a place to hide and spot Julian from the other night chatting up a beautiful brunette at the bar. Letting out a groan, I slide closer to Aldo and hang my head in shame. Ivy's right, I *have* been throwing myself at men, but that's only because Piper promised I would feel better if I did.

'I'm sorry.' Ivy reaches over the table and rubs my arm. 'We're just having a little fun.'

I manage a small nod and will the ground to swallow me up.

'Besides, you were only together for five minutes. You must be over him by now?'

I look into her huge eyes and feel my heart pang. I want to tell her that I haven't even come close to being over him. I want to tell her that even the mention of his name makes me feel like I am being stabbed repeatedly. I want to tell her that the thought of him contacting her for any reason whatsoever physically pains me, but instead, I just take a deep breath and tear my eyes away from hers.

'Of course, I'm over him.' I mutter, fighting to keep a positive expression on my face.

'Finally!' Zara lets out a cheer and raises her glass in the air. 'It's about bloody time!'

Not knowing what to say next, the four of us sit in silence until the sound of Ivy's phone ringing breaks the ice.

'That will be Piper!' Zara claps her hands together excitedly as Ivy runs into the gardens to answer the call. 'She must be on her way!'

Before I can speak, Aldo lets out a huge yawn and motions for me to drink up. 'Well, we should be going.' Pushing out his chair, he waits for me to gather my belongings.

'Already?' Zara exclaims, squinting at her watch. 'But you just got here?'

Giving her a look that tells her exactly why we're leaving, Aldo gives the barman a wave and makes for the door. Quickly finishing my drink, I smile apologetically at Zara and hurry after Aldo.

'Do you have to be like that?' I hiss, following him along the dark street. 'Why are you always so rude to my friends?'

'Those women are *not* your friends, Sadie.' Immediately lighting up a cigarette, Aldo holds out his arm for mine.

'Of course, they're my friends! Apart from you, they're all that I have!' Feeling a little defensive over my girls, I shoot him a scowl as we come to a stop outside another bar. 'They don't mean any harm. You just don't understand their humour.'

He sneers and blows a stream of smoke into the cold air. 'Well, with friends like that you certainly don't need any enemies.'

Deciding it's not worth an argument, I choose to drop it and bite my lip. I understand Aldo's dislike of Piper. Let's face it, she isn't exactly known for having a big circle of chums, but Ivy and Zara are alright, aren't they?

'Why do you think Spencer contacted Ivy?' I whisper, not realising until it's too late that I'm thinking out loud.

Aldo checks his phone and shrugs. 'It wouldn't surprise me if *she* was the one contacting *him*.'

'Why would she do that?' I ask, doing a little jog on the spot to keep warm. 'She's only met him a handful of times. They've barely spoken two words to one another.'

'Well, I wouldn't put it past her. She'd do anything for a bit of attention...' He looks deep in thought and takes another drag.

She wouldn't do that. Surely not. Before I can stop it, images of the pair of them spring into my head. I picture them rolling around in his bed, sweaty and hot with lust. My stomach flips and a wave of nausea runs through me.

I'd almost convinced myself that Spencer had died. That he had never existed in the first place and was just a figment of my over-active imagination. A lump forms in my throat as I recall boarding that train for the final time. Sometimes I think if it wouldn't have been for that damn tattoo, we would still be together.

With us deciding against the tradition of an engagement ring, Aldo decided to buy me a tattoo on my ring finger as an alternative. I loved the idea straight away. It was so me, so us and everything we stood for. I was so high on adrenaline that I didn't even notice the pain of the needle as it dragged through my skin. All I could think about was Spencer and how happy he was going to be when he saw it.

As soon as we stepped out of the studio, I jumped on the next train to Brighton. I had a few cocktails on the journey, which made the long ride down there flash by in a tipsy haze. I ran so fast from the train station that my feet burned like hot lava by the time I arrived at his door. Rapping on the knocker, I held my breath as I waited for him to answer. The way that his brow furrowed when he saw me standing there made me realise immediately I had made a massive mistake.

'Surprise!' I yelled, throwing my arms around him and burying my face into his hair.

'What... what are you doing here?' He asked, an edge to his voice that I hadn't heard before. 'You weren't supposed to be here until Friday.'

'I wanted to surprise you!' I managed, my mouth stretched into a giant smile. 'I've got something to show you!'

Waiting for him to invite me inside, my smile faltered when I realised that he wasn't budging.

'What's wrong?' I asked, suddenly feeling a little uneasy.

Not bothering to disguise the look of annoyance on his face, he begrudgingly stepped aside and closed the door behind me. Still fuelled by alcohol, I ran into the living room and threw myself onto the couch. Carefully taking a seat next to me, Spencer scratched his stubble and exhaled loudly.

'Look what Aldo bought me for my birthday...' Holding out my hand, I spread my fingers to reveal the new inking. 'Isn't it amazing? It's to mark our engagement. You know, since we're not getting a ring...'

His face turned white and I could practically see the blood drain from his cheeks. 'Why... why have you done that?' He managed, refusing to look me in the eye.

The anger in his voice seemed to sober me up in an instant.

'You seem mad...' I whispered, edging closer to him. 'What's wrong?'

'What's wrong?' He repeated, laughing sarcastically. 'Sadie, *all* of this is wrong! You, the tattoo, the whole engagement thing...'

Seemingly losing the ability to speak, I stared at him in shock. I felt like I had been slapped. My skin burnt from his sharp tongue, making me numb from head to toe. I sat there, glued to the couch as he paced up and down the living room.

'Things are moving too fast for me. I was never looking for anything serious, but then I met you and things just spiralled out of control.' Leaning against the doorframe, he let out a groan and stared down at the ground. 'I'm just not ready to settle down. I thought I was, but I'm not.' Turning to face me, he finally got the courage to look me in the eye. 'I don't know what to say. I'm sorry.'

His words made me dizzy as I repeated them over and over in my mind, not once believing that they were true. I felt paralysed as I waited for him to laugh and say that he was playing the world's cruellest joke.

Looking back, I don't know why I didn't flip, why I didn't freak out or erupt into a fit of rage. Instead, I simply picked up my bag and walked out of the door. He shouted after me, but I didn't look back. I just continued to put one foot in front of the other in a dazed haze until I reached the train station. The entire hour I waited for a train to come by, I looked over my shoulder and prayed that he would come after me. I ached for him to pull up in his car and tell me he had made a terrible mistake. I would have given anything to hear him say that he didn't mean a single word he had said.

Of course, that never happened. It never does in real life, does it? That final *I'm sorry* he yelled as I disappeared down his path are the last words he ever said to me. I never found out what it was that made Spencer cut me off like that and I guess I never will. They say, *what you don't know doesn't hurt you*, but not knowing why I was treated so badly by the only person I've ever loved has haunted me since that fateful day.

Sometimes I ask myself what's worse, knowing how badly you want something, or knowing that you can never have it?

Chapter 7

Sunlight floods the room as I run my legs over the soft sheets and inhale deeply. Slowly peeling open my eyes, I close them again as the familiar feeling of dread hits my stomach. I've tried to keep a strong front in place, but inside I am starting to crumble. With each day that passes I can feel the mask slipping more and more. It's just a matter of time before someone points out the cracks in my positive exterior.

Blinking as I let out a yawn, I roll onto my side and stare out of the window. Fluffy clouds hang perfectly in the blue sky, tickling the tops of the trees in the distance. Hugging the pillow tightly, I have an overwhelming urge to tug the duvet over my head and pretend that today has been cancelled. When I felt down as a child, a simple bar of chocolate and an Enid Blyton book was all it took to lift my spirits. A smile plays on the corner of my lips as I remember the days where my biggest worry was getting my homework in on time. If only all of life's problems could be solved with a simple sugar hit.

Hearing voices in the living room, I grab my dressing gown from the back of the door and rub last night's mascara from beneath my eyes.

'What's going on out here?' I ask, smiling as I open the door to reveal Aldo and Edward sprawled out on the couch.

'We're arguing!' Edward declares, giving Aldo a playful nudge. 'Can you please tell him that *honey* is not an acceptable colour for a bathroom?'

'Honey?' I frown and flick on the coffee machine. 'What are you talking about?'

Edward looks at Aldo to elaborate, but he simply shakes his head and looks down at the floor guiltily. Taking a mug from the cupboard, I look between the two of them and wait for an explanation.

'Well, what's going on?' I offer Aldo a smile, but he just stares back at me uneasily.

'You had to tell her sooner or later.' Edward gives Aldo's arm a squeeze and I feel a wave of worry.

Clearing his throat, Aldo runs his fingers through his hair and attempts to keep his voice light. 'The thing is, Edward and I are considering moving in together.'

'Considering?' Edward interjects, shooting Aldo daggers. 'We've just picked out paint samples!'

Ignoring the sadness in my chest, I keep smiling and pray that my true feelings don't show. 'That's great news! I'm so happy for you both!'

'You are?' Aldo mumbles uncertainly, bringing his eyes up to mine. 'I was a little worried about how you would take it.'

'Don't be silly!' I fire back, leaning over the couch and embracing them both warmly. 'It's about time you flew the nest.'

Aldo gives me a look which says he doesn't believe me and I pretend I haven't noticed. I knew that Aldo and I couldn't live together forever. Eventually one of us would become a fully certified grown up and join the real world. I just didn't see it happening anytime soon, that's all. They have only been together for two minutes and for at least one of those minutes they've been at one another's throats.

Turning my attention to the coffee maker, I leave the two of them to discuss colour charts and pop a couple of slices of bread into the toaster. I can't let Aldo see that I am upset. It wouldn't be fair of me to ruin this monumental step in his relationship with my own selfish feelings.

'Do you want to come to Ikea with us?' Edward asks, reaching for his coat.

I envisage the three of us walking around the iconic furniture store and cringe. My gay best friend, his boyfriend and me. Pathetic just doesn't cover it.

'Thanks for the offer, but I've got to check on my mum's house. She's gone to Dubai for a little while.' Hopping onto a stool, I cradle the hot mug close to my chest.

'Well, you know where we'll be if you change your mind.' Grabbing Aldo by the sleeve, Edward turns on his heels and immediately starts talking about kitchen appliances.

Watching the door slam behind them, I rest my elbows on the breakfast bar and sigh. I need to get my life back on track. Even Aldo is moving forward and making plans for the future. Two months post-breakup and I'm still moping around, still unable to close the door and move on. If losing my contract with Precious wasn't enough to give me a reality check, then I really am heading for trouble.

I've always believed that when one door closes another one opens, but lately I feel like I've had one door after the next slam in my face. First Spencer and now Precious. If bad things come in threes, I dread to think what is next...

* * *

Pulling up outside my mother's extravagant abode, I turn off the engine as the gates automatically close behind me. Looking up at the house before me, I pause to check out the fleet of extravagant sports cars. Red, yellow, green and blue, all neatly lined up in front of the garages. In true Mick style, he chooses to leave his prized toys in full view of the passing public. *Some things are supposed to be admired*, he so often tells me, not caring in the slightest that they're just an open invitation to be stolen.

Sliding my key into the lock, I'm surprised to notice that she's decorated again. My mother's constant need to redecorate means that her house is so unfamiliar to me. Each time I come here it looks completely different to the last.

Stepping into the hallway, my eyes scan the open space cautiously. The old building has been thoroughly renovated, not a hint of the original interior remains. When she first bought this place, it was like a little piece of history. Coming here used to feel like you were stepping back in time. I hardly recognise it since Mick got his grubby hands on the keys. Gone are the wooden beams, the period-style drapes and the ornate fireplaces that warmed every room.

Today the house is a boring shade of magnolia, with a glass frontage and more diamantes than you could ever imagine. There's not a hint of my mother to be seen.

Wandering around the living room, I cast my eyes over the many photographs that adorn the marble mantelpiece. There must be fifty pictures here and I'm not on a single one of them. From exotic images of the many idyllic islands they have visited over the years, to Mick's litter of children, they're all displayed proudly for the world to see.

I pick up a gold frame and stare at the unfamiliar faces looking back at me. Mick has six children to six different women, none of which he has any contact with. Well, unless you count sending a gift voucher in the mail every Christmas as *contact*. Mum won't address the issue. The one time I tried to bring it up she completely flipped out and told me to mind my own business. Personally, I don't think his six abandoned children would be as protective over her beloved Mick.

Putting down the frame, I pad into the kitchen and look up at the giant chandelier overhead. It's such a bizarre feeling to not recognise your own mother's home. To be completely honest, using the word *mother* feels foreign to me, too. She's always been more like a distant friend or an older sister who only acknowledges me because she feels morally obliged.

You're probably wondering why I'm being so blasé about this, but the truth is, I accepted my strained relationship with my mum a long time ago. Having Aldo by my side over the past few years has made it easier to deal with. He filled my mother's shoes better than she ever could.

A pang of sadness hits my stomach as I am reminded that he will soon be leaving me. Unintentionally, I have been using Aldo as a crutch to get over Spencer. Since our breakup, I haven't spent a single night alone. It's been Aldo and I through it all. Chick flicks, ice-cream and booze-fuelled dinners that resulted in us dancing the night away until the early hours.

A part of me is worried that once he is gone, I will start the grieving process all over again. After all, you've never truly grieved for something, until you have grieved alone...

Chapter 8

'Did I tell you he has a *yacht* in Monaco?' Piper teases, twirling a pile of tagliatelle with her fork and raising her eyebrows. 'He's offered to take me there next week!'

Responding with a nod, I shoot a glance at Ivy. All evening she has been glued to her phone, giggling like a teenager as she clacks at the keyboard. Catching me looking at her, she quickly shoves the handset into her handbag and motions for Piper to tell her more.

'He also owns a fleet of private jets and like, a *million* properties...' Piper's eyes sparkle and I can almost see pound signs floating around her head.

'So...' I interrupt, hoping that she doesn't bite my head off. 'Does anyone else have anything to share?' I feel Piper's eyes burning into me and pretend I haven't noticed. 'Anything at all?'

Hoping that the twins have also tired of the sound of Piper's voice, I send them a mental SOS to change the subject.

'Word on the grapevine is that Aldo's moving out...' Zara puts down her fork and pushes away her plate. 'What happened there?'

'Jeez, Sadie! You can't even keep a *gay* man!' Piper throws back her head and laughs manically. 'I'm kidding!' She adds, clearly sensing I'm a little stung.

Biting my lip, I look down into my salad and try not to retaliate.

'Oh, come on!' Piper presses, sipping her mineral water. 'You've got to admit it's a little funny.'

'First Spencer and now Aldo!' Zara howls and bangs her fist down on the table. 'What do you do to these guys?'

The three of them burst into hysterics and I force myself to join in. I don't think anyone could understand how devastated I am at Aldo moving out, but I refuse to let it show. They don't understand the connection that Aldo and I have, no one does.

Clearing my throat, I put down my fork and focus on Ivy. 'Speaking of Spencer, did you ever find out why he was contacting you?' My heart pounds in my chest as the table falls into an uncomfortable silence. 'What?' I mumble, taking in their guilty faces anxiously.

Piper and Zara exchange glances as Ivy's cheeks turn a bright shade of pink.

'Let's not make a big deal out of this, okay?' Piper exclaims, tossing her hair over her shoulder dramatically. 'Spencer and Ivy have been talking.'

'Talking?' I whisper, praying that I've got the wrong end of the stick. 'Why?'

Ivy fidgets nervously and looks away, not breathing a word. Realising that my suspicions are right on the money, my jaw drops open in shock.

'Oh, don't look like that, Sadie!' Piper scoffs in annoyance, rolling her eyes. 'You guys were together for two bloody minutes!'

Every hair on my body stands to attention as I try to process what she is saying. *Ivy and Spencer?* I look around the table and pray to wake-up from this nightmare, but the three faces just stare back at me blankly.

Feeling tears prick at the corners of my eyes, I grab my jacket and throw some notes down on the table. 'I've got to go...' I stammer, suddenly having the overwhelming urge to vomit. 'I need to get out of here.'

Squeezing through the sea of tables, I force myself to keep it together until I make it out onto the street. *Talking?* The word sounds so innocent, but we all know exactly what it means. How could he do this to me? How could *Ivy* do this to me? My chest becomes painfully tight as I fight back the tears.

Whilst I have spent the last couple of months struggling to get over Spencer, he has been trying to get into my friend's pants. I feel like I've been stabbed, stabbed in the back by people I trusted. How can a few words cause you actual physical pain? A lump forms in my throat as I look left and right before running across the dark street. I will not cry in public. I haven't cried in years and I will be damned if I do it now.

Pulling my jacket tightly around my body, I march past the taxi rank and bury my face in my scarf. The sharp wind bites at my face as my feet pound against the concrete. I don't want to make small talk with a cab driver, I don't want to make small talk with *anyone*. I just want to go home and pretend this whole conversation didn't happen.

I hear laughter and look across the street to see a young couple chasing one another playfully. Happiness beams out of them as they run along the lane and I smile sadly. Why can't I have that? Why have I only ever felt a connection with one guy in twenty-five years and why did he turn out to be such an arsehole? The only opportunity I've ever had to make a family of my own was brutally snatched away from me and I have no idea why.

Continuing towards my apartment, I quicken my pace as heavy rain starts to fall from the sky. The balls of my feet burn as I race along the road in my heels, but it just pushes me to run even faster than I was before. Numerous cars whizz past me, but all I see is a blur of colour. I can't focus on anything else other than getting back to the safety of home. By the time I arrive at the gates, my hair and clothes are completely drenched. Shielding my eyes from the torrential rain, I jog across the car park and practically throw myself inside the building. A few neighbours make attempts to talk to me, but the only person I want to talk to is Aldo.

Wringing the excess water out of my hair, I knock on the door and wait for Aldo to answer. When nothing happens, I let myself in.

The apartment is eerily quiet, indicating that Aldo isn't home. A groan escapes my lips as a handwritten note on the fridge confirms my fears. Leaning over the counter, I tear off the piece of paper and toss it into the bin. Time alone with my thoughts is something I could really do without right now. I need my friend here to help me see this rationally, to stop me from getting hysterical and to give me a much-needed hug.

Walking into the kitchen, I kick off my wet shoes and strip down to my underwear. Spotting Aldo's clean laundry on the couch, I grab one of his tracksuits and tug it on. Stealing Aldo's clothes is another thing I shall miss when he leaves. My stomach flips and I tell myself to pull it together. I just need a plan. A plan that will help me to fill this empty feeling that seems to be getting bigger every day.

What is so fundamentally wrong with me that prevents me from holding down a relationship? And not just with a man, with anyone. My own mother hates me, my best friend doesn't want to live with me anymore and the man I was planning on marrying has his sights set on my mate. My whole life is pathetic. *I* am pathetic.

My head starts to throb and I fumble around in my handbag for my purse. The emergency pack of painkillers I keep hidden behind my bank cards have been used more than ever lately. Fumbling with the zip, I curse under my breath as the entire contents spill out onto the floor. Hastily gathering up my belongings, my fingers land on an ancient sheet of paper that has been folded neatly. Tears spill down my cheeks as I turn it over and stare at the angrily scrawled out name. Gavin Gastrell. One name that means so little, yet so much at the same time. I smooth out the creases and hold the paper against my chest.

Even my dad didn't stick around to get to know me. Sitting cross-legged on the floor, I rest my head against the wall and allow my eyes to close. Before I can stop it, I have images of the man who walked out on my mother before I was born. I picture him teaching me how to ride a bike, throwing me in the air to make me giggle and tickling me under the chin. I envisage us on holiday as a family, smiling as we make sandcastles and squealing as the waves attempt to wash it away. He should have been there. He *could* have been there. To pick me up when I fall, to protect me from making mistakes and to hold me when I get my heart broken.

I have struggled through so many years without him, maybe the next few years would be a whole lot better if I had my father by my side. With a sudden determination, I push myself to my feet and collapse into a chair with my laptop. Before I know what I'm doing, my fingers start to clack away at the keys, frantically scouring all social media platforms for any trace of the name that has haunted me for years. My ears ring as adrenaline soars through my body. Gastrell. It's not exactly a common name, he can't be that hard to find.

Believe it or not, I've never attempted to track down my father before now. The way my mother looked at me when I dared to bring it up was enough to put me off forever.

When both Twitter and Facebook both prove useless, I search the online phone directory in a last-ditch attempt. My hands tremble as I press *enter* to reveal two profiles. One belonging to a Gavin Gastrell in Oxford, estimated to be between the ages of twenty-five and thirty and the other to a man in Manchester. The exact part of Manchester that my mother and I lived before she won the lottery. I check out the age estimation and feel the blood drain from my face. He's between forty and forty-five. It has to be him. It *has* to be. My finger hovers over the record, slightly reluctant to click *view*. Do I really want to do this?

A flashing icon next to his name tells me that they have his full address and phone number available. One click. That's all it will take to reveal everything I have ever wanted to know. Entering my card details, I close my eyes and press the button. The page springs to life and I take a deep breath before opening my eyes. There he is. Gavin Gastrell. A shocked laugh escapes my lips as I take in the address. All this time he has been just forty minutes away. For decades he has been within touching distance and our paths haven't crossed once.

I look up at the clock on the wall as a crazy thought runs through my mind. Not stopping to think about it, I take a screen-shot of the address and grab my car keys.

Taking risks isn't normally my style, but sometimes you just have to take a chance, because you never know how perfect things could turn out...

Chapter 9

Indicating left, I brake gently as the sat nav informs me I have reached my destination. You would think the long drive over here would be enough to make me come to my senses, but I'm more determined than when I left home earlier. I feel full of hope that this is the answer to my problems. If I can forge a meaningful relationship with my dad, it would put everything else in the shadows. A relationship that will stand the test of time and not leave me feeling like an inconvenience or a burden when the going gets tough.

Turning onto a quiet avenue, I turn down the radio and pull up onto the kerb. I squint at the house numbers in search of thirty-nine as a black estate car drives past me and stops in front of the exact house I'm looking for. Shrinking down into my seat, I pull my hood over my head and tug on the drawstring as the doors open and out step three pairs of feet. The first pair belong to a boy. He's tall and slim, like me, with a head of mousey curls. Tugging a backpack onto his shoulder, he makes his way along the path and opens the front door.

Watching him with my mouth wide open, I almost miss the pretty blonde women giggling as they link arms and follow the boy inside the house. They look so similar, they must be mother and daughter. One by one, lights appear in the windows as they make themselves at home.

'Gavin!' One of the blonde women shout from inside the house. 'Don't forget to bring the shopping in from the boot.'

A shadow in the car nods and I feel my heart pound in my chest.

I wasn't expecting this. Well, I don't exactly know what I was expecting, but this wasn't it. He has a whole new life. He has a proper family. He's moved on.

The sound of a car door slamming makes me visibly jump as the driver's door swings open. Holding my breath, I stare at the man whose genes I am made up of. I don't recognise him. I always thought that I would if I ever saw him, but this man could be anyone. He's not that tall, has thinning hair and extremely heavyset shoulders. He looks so much younger than the man I pictured. Granted he is only sixteen years older than me, but I thought he would be more dad-like. Older, wiser and most certainly more familiar. He is literally ten feet away from me, but he couldn't look less familiar if he tried.

Leaning on the steering wheel for a closer look, I pull down my hood and press my face against the windscreen. Accidentally hitting the horn, I swear out loud as Gavin turns around and stares right at me. Completely paralyzed with fear, I freeze in my seat as he closes the driver's door and makes his way over to my car.

Not daring to breathe, I stare directly ahead as he taps on the window. With trembling fingers, I press the controls and slowly turn my head to face him.

'Are you alright?' He asks, in a thick Manchester accent. 'You know there's no through road down here anymore, don't you?'

Staring into his eyes, eyes that feel completely alien to me, I resort to a slow shake of the head. There's just nothing, no connection, no emotion. How can he not know who I am? I am inches from his face and he doesn't have a clue of my identity. I told you earlier about my secret fantasy, the one where my dad has always watched me from afar? Well, now it's pretty obvious it was exactly that, a fantasy. Nothing more, nothing less. This man doesn't have a pang of unexplained fatherly love for me. He just thinks I'm a rather suspicious looking woman sat in a hoody and casing his house.

Starting to walk away, he pauses in the middle of the road before coming back towards me. Every muscle in my body stiffens as he pulls his brow into a frown.

'Are you *sure* you're alright?' Leaning into the car, he squints at me with a concerned expression on his face.

This man isn't who I'm looking for. I can feel it inside. Gate-crashing his family for absolutely no reason is not the answer to my problems. It isn't going to make me happy or give me the fulfilment I need, it's just going to open a can of worms that will be impossible to close.

'I'm fine.' I fire up the engine and release the handbrake. 'Thank you for asking.'

Smiling back at me, he taps his hand on the bonnet and steps to the side as I do a quick U-turn in the street. Not looking back, I put my foot on the accelerator and fire off into the distance. A sense of emptiness settles over me as the sat nav directs me back home. I haven't wanted to admit it to myself, but it doesn't feel like home anymore. They say home is where the heart is, only my heart has been hollow for quite some time.

Spencer broke me. He actually broke my heart in two, but in true Sadie style, I had to hide the way I feel from the world. The longer I kept it inside, the easier it became to ignore, but now all the pain I have kept buried is making a bid for freedom. It wants to be heard. It wants to be acknowledged.

I've tried to throw myself into my work, but even that has fallen flat. All my efforts to create a solid reputation as an artist have boiled down to an apology and a list of possibilities. Possibilities which never materialised. I'm a failure. Every aspect of my life is falling apart. I've buried my head in the sand and tried to pretend that it isn't happening, but the truth is, this isn't a dress rehearsal.

I can't hit rewind and start all over again. I can't fast forward to the point where everything falls into place. This is my life and right now, I don't know whether I want to fight for it anymore...

THE EYE OF THE TORNADO

Chapter 10

I haven't slept all night, not even for an hour. My pillow is saturated with tears, my face hurts from crying and my body physically aches. I feel so empty, so low and just so worthless. Since I arrived back at the apartment yesterday evening, I've had an awful churning in my stomach, a sensation of dread I just can't explain. At first, I thought it was the shock of coming face-to-face with my biological father, but that's not it. Discovering my dad has a whole new family is just the tip of the iceberg.

Feeling tears prick at the corners of my eyes once more, I curl up into the foetal position and try to shut out the world. I have nothing to get up for. No fiancé, no job, no roommate. No one is going to miss me for just one day. Grabbing my phone from the bedside table, I hold my finger on the *off* button until the screen bounces to black. I don't want to be bothered by anyone today. For the next twenty-four hours, I just want to be alone.

Letting out a silent sob, I bury my face into the pillow and wrap my arms around my knees. My chest feels heavy as I squeeze my eyes tightly shut, desperately wanting to disappear into the soft duvet.

'Shirley?' I hear the door squeak open and Aldo's voice drift inside. 'Shirley, are you here?'

Reluctantly poking my head out of the sheets, I force a smile and push myself into a sitting position.

'Heavy night?' Raising his eyebrows at my appearance, he throws himself onto the bed and produces a brown paper bag.

'I'm not hungover...' I manage, shaking my head as he offers me a plastic box.

'You're kidding, right? I walked all the way from Edward's place for this!' Aldo tears off the paper and hands me a plastic fork. 'Eat it.'

Begrudgingly accepting the box, I look down at the avocado and eggs sceptically.

'You look like shit.' He remarks, grabbing a pillow and wedging it behind his head. 'What did you do last night?'

'I went to see my dad...' I reply, not a hint of emotion in my voice.

Pausing with a bagel halfway to his mouth, Aldo stares at me incredulously. 'What the hell are you talking about?'

Really not wanting to discuss it, I take a tiny bite of grilled bread and turn away from him.

'Shirley?' Aldo persists, his eyes wide with shock.

Realising that he isn't going to drop it, I lick my dry lips before responding. 'He didn't know who I was. It's not a big deal...'

'It's a huge deal!' He whispers, clearly shocked to the core. 'Why didn't you say anything?'

Shrugging my shoulders, I push the box away and sigh heavily. 'I don't really know. I guess I just had a yearning.'

'You should have told me!' Aldo's brow creases into a frown as he polishes off the last of his breakfast. 'How do you feel?'

'I don't really feel anything. He was just a guy. I won't be going back. I just want to draw a line under it and move on.' Suddenly remembering I have last night's makeup on, I reach for my cleanser and make an attempt at changing the subject.

'So, you're moving in with Edward?' I grab a mirror and rub at my eyes with a cotton pad.

'Listen, Shirley, I didn't want you to find out like that.' Aldo drops the now empty paper bag into the bin and rolls onto his side, studying my face carefully. 'Are you *sure* you're okay with me leaving, because you know you can tell me if you're not?'

'Of course, I am okay with it!' I reply enthusiastically, silently begging him not to go. 'I'm very happy for you.'

'Nothing will change.' He leans across and tickles me playfully. 'We will still hang out all the time. I'll only be a phone call away...'

Managing a sad smile, I nod in response and try not to tear up again. 'Like I said, I'm happy for you...' Unable to stop it, my voice trails off into a series of sobs as Aldo looks at me in bewilderment.

'What's with you today?' He laughs nervously and pulls me towards him. 'Hey, I saw Ivy in the village...' Aldo twists my hair off my face and reaches for his mobile. 'Why don't I give her a call and see if she wants to come over? That might cheer you up a little...'

'No!' I yell, louder than I intend to. 'Do *not* call Ivy!'

Last night's events hit me like a blow to the stomach as Aldo waits for me to elaborate, a bewildered expression on his face. 'What's going on with Ivy?'

Holding my head in my hands, I try to play it down. 'It's Spencer...'

'Spencer?' He interrupts, even more confused than he was a moment ago. 'What's Spencer got to do with Ivy?'

'They've been *talking*...' The words make me wince as I spit them out.

It turns out that I don't need to say another word, as the look on his face tells me he knows exactly what I mean.

'You've got to be kidding me?' Aldo's voice is thunderous as he sits bolt upright. 'I leave you for one night and all hell breaks loose! What the hell are they playing at?'

My cheeks flush as blood rushes to my face in embarrassment. 'They're both adults. They're both single. Just leave them to it. I don't want to say another word about it...'

Aldo doesn't respond and as a result, we fall into an unbearable silence. This is exactly what I didn't need today. Just as I am about to suggest that Aldo leaves me alone for a little while, he clears his throat and stands to his feet.

'Let's go for a walk.' Tossing me a towel, he disappears into my bathroom and turns on the shower.

'I don't want to go for a walk.' I grumble, recognizing that I am on the verge of tears once more.

'I don't care.' With a stern scowl, he flicks on the light and ushers me into the en-suite. 'Get in the shower, you can't go out in public looking like that.'

Not being able to argue with the fact that I look like death, I roll out of bed and grab some clean clothes from the wardrobe. I've known Aldo for long enough to know that he won't give up and leave me alone. I might as well just pacify him and get it over with.

'Give me ten minutes.' I grumble, slipping inside the bathroom and letting the door close behind me.

The sound of water thundering out of the shower head drowns out his response as I strip down to my birthday suit. Grabbing a hair tie, I catch my reflection staring solemnly back at me in the mirror. My eyes are red from crying and the dark circles beneath them age me by at least ten years. Taking a step closer, an image of my dad flashes through my mind. I don't look anything like him. Taking in my facial features, I try to find even a slight resemblance to the man I saw yesterday.

Eventually giving up, I stick a hand under the running water before stepping inside the cubicle. My muscles automatically tense up as the powerful stream pummels into my skin. Tilting back my head, I allow the water to wash over me before it crashes down onto the tiles.

A small tornado forms around the plug hole and I find myself hoping beyond hope that it would take my anguish with it...

Chapter 11

Branches crunch below my feet as I follow Aldo's trail in the mass of brown leaves covering the ground. Due to the sudden drop in temperature, there's no one else around, resulting in Aldo and I having the entire forest to ourselves. The bare trees tremble in the wind as I bury my face into the collar of my coat for warmth. During the summer months, this is one of my favourite places in the world, but when raindrops are landing on your nose it doesn't quite have the same effect.

Pausing for breath, I spot Aldo ahead and raise my hand in acknowledgment. He smiles broadly and flashes me the thumbs-up sign. Continuing up the hill, I shove my hands in my pockets and try to pull myself together for Aldo's sake. He has tried so hard to cheer me up, I can't bring myself to admit that I feel worse than I did last night. I might have managed to fix my face into something that resembles a smile, but inside my heart is hurting.

'It's beautiful, isn't it?' Aldo points to the magnificent view below as I come to a stop next to him.

Nodding in response, I take in the scene in front of me. A sea of green stretches out as far as the eye can see, gently kissing the rolling hills in the distance. The cloud-covered sky wraps the panoramic vista in a protective blanket, shielding it from the rest of the world.

Dropping my backpack, I sit cross-legged on the rock and take a deep breath. Usually this blows me away, but today I just feel empty. It's like its lost its magic, its shine. Beauty is all around me, but I just can't bring myself to appreciate it. Not the mountain of fallen leaves, not the sprawling landscape, not even the sight of birds dancing overhead can bring me to smile and mean it.

I catch Aldo looking at me warily and pretend I haven't noticed. He has been staring at me with the same look of worry in his eyes all morning.

'Are you feeling any better?' He asks gently, sitting down next to me.

Not wanting to discuss how I feel, I take a bobble from my wrist and gather my hair into a ponytail. 'I was fine this morning and

I am fine now.' A wave of hurt hits his eyes at my dismissive tone and I immediately feel guilty. 'Sorry.' I add, turning to face him. 'I don't know what's come over me today.'

Checking out his black manicure, Aldo casts his eyes over the incredible view. 'It's okay to be upset, you know? You don't have to keep things bottled up all the time.' He pauses for effect as a flock of birds soar in the distance. 'You've been through a lot lately. Spencer, Precious, your dad...'

Not wanting to go over the disaster that is my life again, I exhale loudly and scowl. 'You don't have to make it sound so dramatic, Aldo. I've been through a breakup. Big deal. Relationships end all the time. You just have to pick yourself up and move on. The same goes for Precious. It's not the end of the world.' Aldo doesn't say a word, so I carry on talking. 'And as for my dad, well, you can't lose something you never had, can you?'

The thing is, I genuinely don't feel like I'm all that bothered by the events of late. Obviously, they have upset me. Spencer nearly broke me completely, but I will dust myself down. Tomorrow's a new day, life moves on. The sun will still rise and people will continue with their lives. No one cares that a woman has had her heart broken, in theory lost her job and discovered her dad has a whole new family she isn't part of. There are people who have lost loved ones, had life-changing surgery and are facing painful medical treatment. How dare I act like the injured party when there are real problems in the world?

The aching sense of dread that tormented me all night makes a return and I breathe deeply in a bid to expel it from my body.

'I just want you to know that I'm here if you ever want to talk about anything...' Aldo picks up a stone and tosses it over the edge skilfully. 'You know I'm not one for deep and meaningful chats, but you get what I'm saying.'

Not daring to look at him in case I lose control of my emotions, I give him a small nod and stare straight ahead. Leaning back onto the rock, I look over my shoulder as a rustling comes from between the trees. Quickly spotting a fluffy puppy delightfully diving into a pile of leaves, I roll onto my stomach to watch him play. His tail wags furiously as he bounds up and down like a pogo stick, barking happily at his owner.

We could learn a lot from our canine friends. The consistently cheerful animals who find joy everywhere they go make us humans pale in comparison. Digging up a mound of soil, he picks up a branch with his teeth before firing back through the trees. I keep my eyes fixed on him until he disappears out of sight, wondering if I can find it in myself to be that happy.

'I guess we should head back.' Aldo clears his throat and holds out a hand to help me to my feet. 'It's starting to rain again.'

Dusting myself down, I link my arm through his as we retrace our steps through the woods. Despite my initial protest at leaving the apartment, now that I am out in the open I really don't want to go back. If it wasn't for the rain I would stay here all day, anything to not be cooped up with my thoughts.

'Do you have any plans later?' I ask, hoping that we can do something to take my mind off things.

Digging his cigarettes from his back pocket, he nods as he lights up. 'I'm going to start moving some of my stuff out tonight.'

'Already?' I gasp, feeling genuinely shocked. 'Why the rush?'

'Why wait?' He fires back, apparently not realising how mortified I am. 'You can give us a hand, if you want?'

Knowing that I will only spend the evening crying into Aldo's belongings, I shake my head and say nothing. Moving in with a partner is a momentous occasion in anyone's life. He doesn't need my negativity ruining it for him. Telling myself I'll go back to my original plan of hiding beneath my duvet for the day, I give Aldo's arm a squeeze and plant a kiss on his cheek.

'Enjoy your evening with Edward. I wish you all the luck in the world...'

* * *

Laughter floats into the bedroom and I turn up the television in a bid to drown it out. I should be in there. I should be helping my best friend start this new chapter in his life. Instead, I am crashed out in bed, watching TV shows I have seen ten times already. What is wrong with me? For a moment, I consider forcing myself out of bed, but something stops me. I don't quite know what, but I can't bring myself to join in with the jovialities. I feel like someone has turned off my happiness switch today. My default setting appears to be, well, I don't think I have an emotion today. I just feel... *nothing*.

Hearing my door creak open, I squeeze my eyes shut and pretend to be sound asleep.

'Sadie?' Aldo whispers, leaning over the bed to check if I am awake.

'Is she asleep?' Edward's voice pipes up in the background as he pops his head into the bedroom.

Aldo takes a step closer and brushes my hair out of my face. 'Yeah, she's out for the count.'

'Shouldn't you wake her and tell her you're leaving?'

There's a long pause before Aldo exhales loudly. 'No. Sleep will do her good. I'll call her in the morning.'

The two of them whisper quietly, before slowly slipping away. Waiting until I hear the front door bang shut before daring to move again, I sit up straight and rub my sore head. I thought a day spent moping would get all of this negativity out of my system. I thought it would help me to see things more clearly and enable me to attack tomorrow with a fresh determination. Unfortunately, all I have done is given myself time to overthink things and worry over everything from Spencer to my lack of income. Every time I think about it I get this all-encompassing sense of queasiness, one which makes me want to put on my trainers and run as far away from reality as possible.

My phone pings and I search through the bedding to locate the handset. Blinking to help my eyes adjust to the bright light, I take in the words on the screen.

Hey!
We're going to The Allotment for dinner.
Want to join us?
Ivy
xoxo

A wave of nausea runs through my veins and I slip my phone under the pillow. The thought of spending another evening listening to Piper and Zara tease me about Spencer going after Ivy is enough to push me over the edge. I can't stop them from dating, but I can spare myself from the hell of having to hear about it.

Throwing my legs over the edge of the bed, I groan as my feet hit the cold floor and wander into the living room. A shocked gasp escapes my lips as I take in the bare area. When he said, he was making a start on moving his things, I thought he meant the odd jumper and maybe a pair of hair straighteners, but he's taken everything. Not that he isn't entitled to, everything that's missing belongs to him, but there isn't a trace of Aldo left. It's like he was never here. Gone are the photographs, the stash of shoes that permanently resided by the couch and the Yankee candles he insisted on burning almost every night.

My eyes flit to the kitchen island to check for his emergency pack of cigarettes and I'm dismayed to discover they're gone too. Not being able to resist, I turn on my heels and rush over to his bedroom. Pushing open the door, my eyes widen as I realise that apart from his bed, it's completely empty. His awards that adorned the walls have vanished, as has the overflowing wardrobe and the never-ending pile of hair products he *borrows* from work. He's really left.

Sitting on the foot of his bed, I look around the room and notice how overwhelmingly tiny it seems now. You would think being empty would have the opposite effect, but the windows seem smaller, the ceiling looks lower and the walls appear to be closing in on me. I suddenly feel a little light-headed as my legs start to tremble. Attempting to keep them still, I push down on my knees with sweaty palms. My heart flutters in my chest as my ears start to ring. Trying to stand up, I collapse onto the bed as my chest becomes painfully tight.

What's happening to me? My head starts to throb as I fight to calm my breathing. I'm having a heart attack. Clutching my chest, I erupt into a series of panic-fuelled sobs. Sweat beads on my forehead as I frantically search my pockets for my mobile. Discovering that it's not there, I reach for the door handle to pull myself up and manage to stumble into my bedroom.

My entire body quivers as I grab my phone and hover a finger over the keypad. The buzzing in my ears stops for a moment and I perch on my dressing table to compose myself.

Dropping my head between my legs, I close my eyes and clutch my racing heart with both hands until it eventually returns to its normal rhythm. When I finally dare to look up, I feel horrendously dizzy. The room is spinning and I feel weaker than I have ever felt before, but I am beyond relieved my heart has stopped pounding.

Not wanting to move in case it starts again, I stiffly put one foot in front of the other and curl up into a tight ball on the bed. I feel paralysed with fear as I try to calm myself down. Wrapping the covers tightly around my body, I sink into the mattress and allow myself to sob. My chest heaves as I gasp for air, letting the tears come harder and faster than they ever have before...

Chapter 12

Tapping my foot impatiently, I chew the inside of my cheek as I wait in line. I've never felt more anxious in my entire life. The moment I opened my eyes this morning, I called my doctor for an emergency appointment. Unfortunately, they were fully booked, which meant that I had two choices, go to the hospital or head to my local chemist for some advice. Given the options available to me, I decided to choose the latter. Only now that I'm here, I don't know what to say.

'How can I help you?' The pharmacist beams brightly and motions for me to step forward.

Being very aware of the long queue behind me, I lower my voice to a whisper. 'I was wondering if you could give me some advice...'

'Of course.' Sensing this is a delicate issue, he whispers to one of the assistants and opens a door behind him. 'Come with me.'

Nodding gratefully, I squeeze past the rows of pills and take a seat in the tiny room. Well, I call it a room, but it's more of a cubicle. It feels cold and clinical, with descriptions of various sexually transmitted diseases on the walls. Feeling highly vulnerable, I pull my handbag onto my lap as the pharmacist sits on the chair opposite and waits for me to speak.

'I... I think I had a heart attack last night.' I mumble, realising that those words sound ridiculous coming out of a healthy young woman's mouth.

'Okay...' He replies slowly, not seeming convinced in the slightest. 'And why do you think that?'

Struggling to maintain my composure, I fidget with the sleeve of my jacket as I recall my ordeal. 'My legs were shaking, I was sweating profusely, the room was spinning so quickly that I thought I would pass out. I had this awful ringing in my ears, almost like alarm bells going off inside my head.' My eyes well up with tears and I blink repeatedly to stop them from spilling down my cheeks. 'My chest became really tight, like someone was squeezing me from the inside. My head started to pound and I couldn't breathe. I just couldn't catch my breath, it was like I was drowning. It was awful. I really thought I was going to die.'

The pharmacist nods carefully and hands me a tissue from the box on the table. 'Okay, the symptoms you are describing resemble those of a panic attack.'

'A panic attack?' I repeat hesitantly, conjuring up images of stressed mothers breathing into paper bags. 'Are you sure?'

He nods confidently and leans on the plastic table. 'Panic attacks are frequently mistaken for heart attacks. I know this might seem difficult to believe. There's a slight chance the symptoms could be the result of an underlying problem, but given your age and other factors, panic attacks are the most likely issue here.' Reaching behind him, he opens a filing cabinet and hands me a leaflet. 'Everything you need to know about how panic affects the human body is explained in here.'

I take the pamphlet sceptically and run my eyes over the text.

Panic attacks are often connected with key life transitions.
Major stress, the death of a loved one, divorce, or a job loss can also trigger panic attacks.

'Is there anything in your life that could have caused you to have a panic attack?' The pharmacist clicks his pen repeatedly and glances up at the clock on the wall.

If I tell him that my fiancé dumped me and my roommate has decided to move in with his boyfriend, he will probably laugh in my face.

'No...' I mumble, quickly folding the leaflet and shoving it into my pocket.

'In that case, I would strongly recommend you pay a visit to your GP to investigate the root cause of the attacks. In the meantime, I can offer you some herbal medication. The success rate is wildly variable, but they might help to take the edge off.' He nods to confirm this is the end of our conversation and pushes out his chair. 'Is there anything else I can help you with?'

I manage a shake of the head and follow him back out onto the shop floor. A lady at the front of the queue pulls her scarf over her nose as I pass by, clearly not wanting to catch whatever terrible disease she thinks I have. The pharmacist motions to one of his assistants and she leads me over to a stand of brightly-coloured boxes.

Grabbing a varied selection, she talks me through the benefits of each one as she scans them through the till. Too flustered to listen, I exchange the glossy bag for a handful of notes and push my way outside.

Racing back to the safety of my car, I tip out the contents of the bag and take in the products in front of me. A lavender spray, a box of valerian sleeping aids and a tin of emergency pastilles. Not knowing which one to use first, I tear open the packaging on the spray and squirt at the back of my tongue as instructed. Expecting to feel instant relief, I stare at the label in disappointment. I don't feel calm, relaxed or reassured, I feel exactly the same as I did an hour ago, dreadful.

I am about to slip my key into the ignition and drive away when I hear a knocking at the window. Looking up to see Patrick beaming back at me, I frantically clear away the herbal remedies as he opens the door and jumps into the passenger seat.

'Sadie!' He gushes, offering his cheek for a kiss. 'How have you been? I've tried to call you a couple of times, but it went straight to voicemail.'

'Oh...' My faces colours up as I remember turning my phone off yesterday. 'My mobile's been playing up lately.'

'Ah...' Nodding along, he rubs his hands together for warmth. 'How did you get on with the list I gave you? Any luck?'

'I'm afraid not.' I mumble, smoothing down my messy hair. 'But something will come up, I'm sure.'

Patrick smiles and I notice his eyes land on my bag of medication. 'They're for a friend.' I stammer, quickly kicking them under my seat. 'She's been through a tough time...'

I hate lying to people, but at least it's half true.

'You look a little tired, Sadie.' Patrick furrows his brow and looks at me the same way that Aldo did yesterday. 'Is everything okay?'

'Everything's fine!' I try to look confident, but I can't even convince myself, let alone anyone else. 'I just didn't sleep too well last night. Anyway, how are you? How's Precious?'

'I'm good, Precious is good, we're all good.' Patrick laughs tensely and scratches his beard. 'I'm heading to Precious right now if you want to join me for some lunch?

I'll have Mario make the lobster bisque you love! What do you say?'

Mario's lobster bisque has always been my favourite, Patrick knows that, but since the so-called *panic attack,* I haven't been able to eat a thing.

'Sadie?' Patrick presses, tapping me on the arm to regain my attention.

'Thanks for the offer, I really appreciate it...'

'I can sense a *but* coming...' He interrupts playfully, reaching out for the door handle. 'It's fine, maybe another time.' Stepping out of the car, he leans over and kisses my cheek. 'If you change your mind, you know where to find me.'

Giving him a wave, I wait until he disappears down the street before pulling out of the car park. When did I become a liar? Why didn't I take him up on his kind offer? Why couldn't I just admit *I'm* the one who has been feeling pretty low recently? Guilt hits me like a blow to the stomach as I cruise along the road. I guess the real question is, why do I feel like this at all?

Chapter 13

'So, you *are* alive...' Pushing her way into the apartment, Piper screws up her nose as she takes in my bedraggled appearance. 'Well, just about. Why are you dressed like that? You're not still moping over the whole Spencer/Ivy situation, are you? Because I've got to tell you, it's getting boring.'

'It's not that...' I stammer, really wishing that she hadn't come over here uninvited. 'I had a...'

'You've been acting so *weird!*' Piper cuts me off mid-sentence and pulls a bottle of wine from the rack. 'Running out on us like that the other night. Dressing like a homeless person. You're so *touchy* lately.'

Opening a few cupboards, she finally locates the wine glasses on the top shelf. Watching her pour the red liquid, I pull out a stool at the kitchen island and tug the sleeves of my jumper over my hands. As usual, Piper is immaculately made-up, which just makes me feel even more ashamed about the state of my appearance.

'Get that down you.' She instructs, tossing her glossy hair over her shoulder. 'We need to have a chat.'

Dragging the glass towards me, I rub my temples as Piper hops onto a stool.

'What's going on with you?' Her little legs swing back and forth as she raps her nails on the counter. 'If it's not Spencer, then what is it?'

I stare into the glass, already hating this conversation. 'I just feel a little, I don't know, *down* lately...'

'Down?' Piper scowls, not waiting for me to explain. 'I thought you said this wasn't about Spencer?'

'It's *not* about him...'

'Then what is it about?' She narrows her eyes as I try to find the words for how I am feeling. 'Well?'

Struggling to get my mouth to engage with my brain, I shake my head and groan. 'I don't know...'

Exhaling loudly, Piper throws back her wine and shakes her head at me incredulously. 'You need to pull yourself together, Sadie. What the hell have you got to feel *down* about? You have been through a damn breakup. Big deal, who hasn't?'

I want to agree with her, but it doesn't feel as simple as that. I want to tell her about the panic attack and how horrendous it was. I want to tell her I'm petrified it will happen again, but I know without trying that she just won't understand. No one will.

'Sadie, are you even listening to me?' Piper bangs her hand down on the table and I jolt to attention. 'You're freaking me out with your silent act. Can you say something, please?'

I hold my head in my hands and feel the now familiar tightening in my chest. Not again, not now.

'Are you taking drugs?' She hisses, her eyebrows higher than they have ever been.

'No, of course not.' I reply, appalled at the thought of her thinking I'm using.

'So, you're just sad and you have absolutely *no* idea why?' She cackles mockingly and purses her lips. 'Have you gone insane? Is that what this is?'

Silently cursing her into oblivion, I resist the urge to scream out loud. I didn't ask her to come here. Why can't she just leave me alone? Why can't *everyone* just leave me alone? Piper continues talking, but I squeeze my eyes tightly shut and cover my ears. When she finally stops for breath, I look up and slide off my seat.

'I'd like you to leave...' Walking over to the door, I wipe my face and blink back tears. 'I want to be alone for a while.'

'*Excuse me?*' Piper's jaw drops open as she waits for me to correct myself. 'I take time out of *my* day to come over here and check that *you* are alright and you're telling me to leave?'

'I'm sorry....' My voice starts to crack and I pray for the ground to swallow me up.

'You need to sort yourself out.' Clacking over the tiles, Piper curls her lips into a snarl. 'I mean, what do you even want out of life? Because if it's another man, you're not going to get one looking like *that*...'

Turning on her heels, she totters down the lobby and disappears into the lift. Seemingly frozen to the spot, I look down at my tattoo and ask myself the same question. What *do* I want out of life? I thought I wanted a husband, children and a family to call my own, but that idea suddenly seems so outlandish to me. What's the point? If I let myself get attached to people, I will only live in fear that one day they'll leave me, just like everyone else does.

Closing the door, I slump to the floor and glance up at the clock on the wall. Earlier today, I called the surgery and made an appointment for tomorrow morning. It's 2017, if we can perform heart transplants, there must be an instant remedy to stop me from feeling like this. I just need to get through the next twenty-four hours and everything will be fine.

Catching a glimpse of myself in the mirror, I feel a wave of shame. Piper was right, I look a mess. I can't believe I left the house like this. My hair is in desperate need of a wash and my skin is dryer than I have ever seen it. Looking in the direction of the bathroom, I try to summon the energy to put one foot in front of the other and walk the short distance across the lounge. What is wrong with me? Why does washing my hair suddenly feel like climbing Everest?

Forcing myself to my feet, I try to block Piper's words out of my mind. How can I make someone else understand why I feel so low when I don't even know myself? Pushing open the bathroom door, I turn on the taps and grab a random bath bomb from the cabinet. The water glistens beneath the bright lights of the bathroom as I step out of my clothes and wait for the tub to fill. Climbing inside, I wrap my arms around my legs and rest my chin on my knees. The hot water stings my skin as it surrounds my body, but it doesn't hurt, not really. The pain is almost comforting. In an inexplicable way, it makes the ache inside me seem less noticeable.

Lowering myself into the water, I tip back my head and feel my muscles slowly relax. My long hair floats around me, wrapping my body in a protective bubble as I allow my eyes to close. Staying perfectly still, I can almost feel the beat of my heart as water fills my ears and drowns out any noise from the outside world. Suddenly I feel safe, I feel comforted by the weight of the water above me. Taking a deep breath, I pull my head beneath the surface of the water and hold on to the sides of the bath. My heart begins to pound harder and faster in my chest as my body begs me to sit up. Fighting against it until my legs start to shake, I eventually push myself up and gasp for air.

My vision is blurred and my hands are shaking, but I feel more alive than I have done in a long time. I clutch the windowsill as my heart races due to the lack of oxygen in my lungs. Turning off the taps, I notice that my legs are shockingly red from the sweltering temperature of the water. Cold air dances around my wet skin and the lingering sense of doom returns to my stomach.

Silent tears slip down my cheeks, joining the pool of water in the tub. I must have cried a river these past few days and I have a terrible feeling that I'm beginning to drown in it...

Chapter 14

Applying a final layer of lipstick, I blink twice and take in my appearance. It may have taken two hours, but all signs of yet another restless night's sleep are now carefully concealed. The bags under my eyes have been cleverly hidden beneath a thick layer of foundation and the dash of pink on my cheeks has given my face the pop of colour it's been crying out for. As much as I didn't enjoy hearing them, Piper's harsh words yesterday got me thinking. Perhaps if I *look* better, maybe I will start to *feel* better.

Fluffing up my hair, I run my fingers through the curls that took me all morning to produce. The platinum waves frame my contoured face, creating a halo effect under the spotlights. I look fine now, so why don't I feel fine? Leaning towards the mirror, I turn my face from side to side for any evidence of what I am experiencing inside. If you passed me in the street, you would have no idea that I feel so much sadness, so much heartache and fear. I find it hard to believe myself. How can I feel so terribly low, yet look so incredibly normal? It's like I am cheating, acting, playing a role that isn't really me.

In the middle of the night, I convinced myself that Piper was right. I pictured myself dressed to kill, with a sudden strength and determination to fix whatever it is that's making me feel so distant. Just like Superman. Without the costume and cape he is powerless, but as soon as he slips into that blue suit he becomes capable of anything. Only I don't feel like a superhero, I feel like a fraud. Like a clown in fancy dress. I don't feel strong and courageous, I feel emptier than ever. I'm pretending to be something I'm not.

Looking around the car park, I stare at the line of people making their way into the surgery and wonder how many of them are hiding behind a mask of their own. The beautiful woman who is carefully juggling twins? The elderly man who is holding open the door for her? Or the teenage boy with bandages wrapped around his wrists? I guess it's not always black and white, is it?

Stepping out of the car, I beep the lock and follow them inside. The surgery is a dreary shade of beige and dare I say it, a little rough around the edges. Checking my phone has been switched to *silent*, I walk to the glass window as the receptionist looks at me expectantly.

'I have an appointment.' I whisper, being very aware that I am a couple of minutes late. 'It's Sadie Valentine.'

'We're running a little behind schedule.' The receptionist clacks away at her keyboard before pointing to her left. 'Take a seat.'

My heart rate increases as I squeeze onto the only empty seat in the room and try to ignore the strange smell in the air. You know the one. The smell that can only be found in hospitals, dentists and other frightening places where they poke you with sharp instruments. A woman opposite rocks a baby back and forth, worry etched onto her face as the child lets out a series of tiny cries. I glance over at the man next to her and notice him wrap a protective arm around them both.

The door squeaks open as a middle-aged man steps into the waiting room. His arm is in a sling and he has numerous small cuts to his face and chest. Wincing as he paces back and forth, he is clearly in a lot of pain. Taking my phone out of my handbag, I catch a glimpse of my reflection in the black screen. What on earth do I look like? I'm in a room filled with genuinely sick people and I'm dressed like I'm on my way to a photoshoot. This is ridiculous. I shouldn't be here.

I hear a commotion at the reception desk and look up to see an elderly woman with a hacking cough practically begging for an appointment. Clutching her chest, she pours a mountain of pill bottles onto the counter and covers her mouth with a tissue. The receptionist checks her computer once more and shakes her head. Finally giving up, the grey-haired lady takes her trolley and slowly heads back outside.

I should be ashamed of myself. There are people here with actual ailments. People who seriously need medical help. How dare I come in here asking to see a doctor because I had a single panic attack? My head starts to spin as I quickly grab my handbag and dive out of my seat.

Pushing my way to the front of the queue, I rap my knuckles on the glass window frantically. 'Can you cancel my appointment, please? Give it to someone who actually needs it.'

Not stopping to hear her reply, I storm through the lobby and burst out into the car park. Spotting the lady with the trolley making her way towards the bus stop, I run after her and tap her shoulder gently.

'Excuse me…' I sniffle, fighting back tears. 'I think an appointment has just become available.'

'It has?' She manages between coughs. 'Thank you! Thank you so much.'

Watching her disappear inside, I head back to my car and practically throw myself into the driver's seat. Opening the glove compartment, I grab a pack of handwipes and look into the rear-view mirror. I need this off my face. My skin is hot with embarrassment. I've never felt so pathetic in all my life. Scrubbing at my cheeks with the harsh wipes, I don't stop until every last scrap has been removed. My ears start to ring and I feel a surge of fear as I anticipate another panic attack. Don't happen here. Please, do not happen here.

Clutching the steering wheel, adrenaline rushes around my body as I fight against it. Just like last time, sweat beads on my forehead as the world around me starts to spin. Quickly remembering that I have the anti-anxiety medications in my handbag, I fumble with the zip and shove a handful of pastilles into my mouth. The sickly-sweet paste makes my stomach churn as I try to chew through it. Breathing in and out like a robot, I finally manage to return my breathing to a normal rate.

Feeling completely violated, I hold my head in my hands and sob. My entire body shakes as I allow myself to cry. People stop and stare, but I've gone past caring. Resting my head on the steering wheel, I cry until there's not a single tear left in my body. I cry until I no longer know what I am crying about. What is happening to me? Just last week I was fine, I was happy. Well, not *happy*, but I was coping. What has gone so deeply wrong to cause me to crumble like this?

Finally pulling myself together enough to make the short journey home, I sob silently as I let myself back into the apartment.

'Shirley!' Aldo's voice rings out from the balcony and I hastily try to compose myself. 'Woah…' Coming to a stop in front of me, he frowns and motions for me to sit down. 'What's happened?'

Being all cried out I stare back at him in total silence, not knowing what to say.

'Sadie, do you want a...' Edward skips across the living room and trails off as he sees my face. 'Is everything okay?'

Mortified at Edward seeing me like this, I hang my head in shame.

'Shirley...' Taking a seat next to me, Aldo brushes my hair out of my face and I wince at his touch. 'Just give me a nod if you're okay?'

Rubbing my back encouragingly, he pulls Edward to one side. 'I told you she wasn't right...' He whispers, giving me a sideways glance. 'I never should have left her.'

Edward murmurs something that I don't quite hear as the two of them have a hushed conversation.

'I'm going to stay here with her tonight.' Aldo exhales loudly as Edward nods in agreement. 'You should head back. I'll call you later.'

I hear them kiss one another goodbye before Aldo grabs a bottle of water from the fridge and curls up on the floor in front of me. His wavy hair falls in front of his face as he looks me dead in the eye. We must sit in silence for a good half an hour, both of us staring out of the window in a strange bubble.

I try to pinpoint when it was that I started to feel this vacant and detached from reality. Over the past couple of months, I have slowly become more and more empty inside. I'd like to say this is nothing more than the realisation of my breakup hitting me, but deep down I know it is more. Suddenly I feel like there's nothing to live for and I honestly don't know why.

'What happened to your face?' Aldo eventually whispers, turning to face me. 'You look like you've had a bad reaction to something.'

Remembering I scrubbed my face with antiseptic wipes, I place a hand on my cheek and recoil as it burns against my cold hands.

'I wanted to take my makeup off...' I whimper, dropping my head onto my lap.

'Why?' Aldo sounds so bewildered that I almost want to laugh.

'I had a panic attack...' My stomach drops to the floor as the words escape my mouth. 'It was so scary. I was so frightened and afraid...'

Wrapping both arms around me, Aldo squeezes tightly and rests his chin on my head. 'When did you last sleep?'

Sleep? I can't remember when I last slept through the night. Two weeks? Maybe three? Resorting to a shrug of the shoulders, I kick off my shoes as Aldo pulls me off the couch.

'Let's get you to bed.' Slipping an arm around my waist, Aldo leads me to my bedroom.

My bed seems to be the only place I feel safe lately. Everything is fine if I just don't leave my bed. Lowering me down like a small child, Aldo tugs the sheets up to my chin and flicks off the light. I feel his presence behind me, watching my every move as I toss and turn to get comfortable. Hearing him leave, I roll onto my side and watch Aldo's feet pace up and down in the tiny space beneath the door. My ears prick up as I hear tinny voices in the distance.

'Linda, I'm really worried about her...'

'She's acting very, I don't know, strange...'

'She's not eating, she's not sleeping, she's been distant...'

'I don't think it is Spencer. It's more than that. I honestly think she's heading for some sort of breakdown...'

'No, you're not listening...'

'Are you seriously asking if she's checked on your house at a time like this? Is that really all you're concerned about?'

'I'm not trying to ruin your holiday! I just thought that you should know...'

'I'm worried she might do something stupid. She needs you right now!'

'There's only so much I can do on my own...'

'You don't care about anyone but yourself, do you?'

'If you put as much care into your daughter as you do into your suntan, then maybe she wouldn't be in this position right now...'

'The apartment? How many times are you going to play that card? She needs a mother, not your bloody money...'

'You don't deserve her...'

'I'll tell you what, Linda, you go back to your holiday and pretend I never mentioned anything...'

There's a series of bangs before Aldo ends the call and curses loudly. My mother, ladies and gentlemen. Holding my pillow over my ears, I find myself wishing that I wasn't such a burden to everyone. What a failure I am. I just want to go to sleep and never wake-up again. I wonder what it would be like to sleep forever. To close your eyes and fall into a delicious darkness, one that you never need to leave, appeals to me more than anything. There's no alarm clock, no outside world, no responsibilities and nothing to wake-up for. A frisson of longing runs through me as I close my eyes and pray for it to happen. My body craves nothingness, but my mind won't allow it. Every time I try to block out the world, the little voice in the back of my mind reminds me that my life is in tatters.

Opening my eyes, I physically jump as I notice Aldo is now at the side of my bed, staring at me intently.

'What are you doing?' I gasp, genuinely shocked to see him.

Not replying, Aldo pulls a clip out of his hair and shakes his head. 'Don't take this the wrong way, but I think you might need some help…'

'Help?' I repeat, not liking the tone of his voice. 'Help with what?'

Shuffling closer to me, he tucks a stray strand of hair behind his ears. 'You're not *you* at the moment. You've been distant for months. I've known there was something not quite right for a while, but I haven't been able to bring myself to say it. My gut is telling me that we need to look into what is going on with you.'

'I'm fine...' I whisper, knowing that he doesn't believe me. 'I've just been feeling a little down lately, that's all. We're all allowed to feel down now and again, aren't we?'

'Shirley...'

'I'm fine! You were right the other day. I *am* upset about Spencer. I'm heartbroken. I just need a few days to get my head around things.' My voice wavers as I hear myself practically begging him to stop looking at me as though I'm heading for a mental institution. 'I have held it together for months now, I think I'm having a delayed reaction...'

Reluctantly accepting this, Aldo nods and takes my hands in his. 'You would tell me if it was anything more than that, wouldn't you?'

'Of course!' I reply, my cheeks flushing as the lie slips straight out of my mouth.

'Well, until you're feeling okay again, I'm going to crash here...'

'No!' I protest, mortified at the thought of inconveniencing him.

'I'm not arguing about this, Shirley. If a few days is all you need, I will be out of your hair in no time. That's the only way I'm not marching you down to the doctor right now.'

I hesitantly nod in agreement as Aldo claps his hands and shakes off his jacket. 'Alright, if this is a post-breakup breakdown, we're going to handle this how we should have done back then. I'm talking movies, face masks, chocolates... *the works!*'

Running into the living room, he shortly returns with his arms laden with products. I smile gratefully as he fiddles with the DVD player before diving into the bed next to me. Fluffing up his pillow, he presses a series of buttons on the remote control. A few seconds later, Dirty Dancing appears on the screen and Aldo rocks his shoulders in time to the music. Attempting to join in, I rest my head on his chest and pretend to be enjoying myself. I don't deserve Aldo. I don't deserve anyone. Hugging him tightly, I thank the universe for bringing him into my life.

My future might seem bleak right now, but as long as I have Aldo by my side, things can only get better...

Chapter 15

Looking around the crowded café, I try to stop my heart from pounding. The thought of having another panic attack in public makes me want to run back to the safety of my bed and never leave. The outside world suddenly seems so frightening and intimidating to me. Leaving the apartment this morning was one of the hardest things I have done, no matter how much Aldo tried to convince me that everything would be okay.

After our movie last night, Aldo and I talked until the sun came up. We covered everything from my relationship with my mother, to Spencer and even Mick. I'd like to be able to say I feel better after our heart to heart, but I am more terrified than ever before. Not only is my failure to act like a normal person affecting me, it's now affecting those around me.

It was around three o'clock in the morning when Aldo used the *d* word. Hearing him talk about depression made my stomach flip like crazy. I tried to dismiss it, but the more symptoms he reeled off, the more concerned I became that I might actually have it. My skin crawls as I recall the words on the computer screen.

People with depression often feel hopeless, sad, empty and lose interest in things they would normally enjoy.

I glance down at the coffee in front of me and try to pretend that I want to be here. I'm also pretending this is just to do with Spencer, when deep inside I know it's much more than that. It feels scarier and far more complex. Despite Aldo's research, I don't think I'm depressed. Maybe at first, but the hollowness that filled me is now ebbing away and in its place, is a sense of dread, worry and fear of the future.

Aldo continues to reel off an itinerary for the day, but my attention is stolen by the various other customers in the restaurant. There are people from all walks of life. Some young, some old, a few singletons and the odd extended family. A whole variety of people, but each one seems to have their life in order and I'm guessing some of them have been through a whole lot worse than I have.

A pang of anger hits me and I'm suddenly extremely annoyed. What the hell is my problem? My failure to act like a normal person has caused my friend to stage an intervention. He is totally convinced that I have depression. I don't have depression, what's really depressing is this situation right here.

'Eat your breakfast.' Aldo instructs, tapping my plate with his fork. 'You know the rules. No breakfast. No shopping.'

I smile back and pinch my leg beneath the table. I haven't eaten properly in so long, the waistband on my jeans is starting to feel loose. Begrudgingly picking up my fork, I sink the prongs into a slice of smoked salmon and nibble at the edge. My appetite seems to have gone out of the window along with everything else. I feel like I'm acting and the world is my audience. I can't let them know how I really feel in case they label me crazy or depressive.

The fish feels alien in my mouth as I force myself to swallow and pray I don't throw up. I won't let this rough patch define me. I don't need help. I don't have depression, anxiety or any of the other scary words Aldo was spouting last night. I just need to have a positive mental attitude, that's all. It sounds so simple in theory, but as I am finding out, putting it into practice is much harder. Maybe this is how people live their lives, putting on a show just to fit in.

'I'm going to settle the bill.' Pushing away his plate, Aldo adjusts his jeans and makes his way to the bar.

Thankful for a few moments alone to drop the fake smile, I exhale loudly and inadvertently catch the attention of a family at the table on my right.

'Are you alright?' The friendly diner asks, struggling to sit a restless toddler in a highchair.

I immediately freeze, wondering why on earth she is asking me that. I'm fine. I have my makeup on, Aldo has blow-dried my hair. There's nothing about me that says, *I'm on the verge of a nervous breakdown*.

'Yes...' I reply, giving her a quizzical look as she returns to her meal.

Maybe she can see through my act. I look up at the ceiling, half expecting to see a grey cloud hanging above my head or a sign that says, *this woman is depressed, anxiety-ridden and everything else that comes with it*. Butterflies attack my stomach as the awful ringing returns to my ears. My heart beats erratically in my chest and I scan the queue of people for Aldo. Trying to keep calm, I pray that I can shake this off.

Fighting with everything I have, I cover my eyes as dread runs through my veins. Knowing the panic has already taken hold, I dive out of my seat as my vision becomes blurry. *No! No! No!* Fresh air fills my lungs as I push open the door and gasp for breath.

Spotting an empty phone box across the street, I clutch my heart as my chest becomes excruciatingly tight. The door closes behind me, blocking out the outside world and giving me the privacy I require. Attempting to use the breathing techniques advised in the pharmacist's leaflet, I look down at the ground and slowly count to ten.

'Shirley?' A light knocking grabs my attention and I spin around to see Aldo peering through the glass. 'What are you doing?'

Ignoring the sweat that is beading on my forehead, I hastily clear my throat. 'I was making a call...'

Aldo's gaze lands on the mobile phone that is poking out of my pocket. 'And you didn't use your own phone *because...*'

Frantically racking my brains for a suitable lie, I shove the handset into my handbag and laugh nervously. 'The battery died.'

Every muscle in my body tells me to stay in the safety of the phone box, but I somehow muster the strength to pull open the door. Wind whips around my face as I inwardly scream at myself to get it together. I am shopping with my best friend, which is one my favourite things to do. Why do I feel like I am being dragged around a funeral parlour? I watch a trio of women laugh in a coffee shop to our left. Glossy bags sit at their feet as they talk animatedly with their hands. When did that stop being me? *Why* did that stop being me?

Desperately trying to keep it together, I link my arm through Aldo's as he leads me into a department store. The warmth of the heating washes over me as we step inside the familiar building. Members of staff who know us well raise their hands in acknowledgment as we head for the escalators. An array of beauty products glisten beneath the bright spotlights, but I have no desire towards any of them. I have no draw, no longing to approach the things that would normally fill me with joy and happiness.

Letting Aldo drag me towards the shoe section, I feign a smile as he gushes over a pair of sparkly boots.

'Aren't these incredible?' Turning over the shoes in his hands, Aldo points to the label and nods appreciatively. 'I just *love* Suave.'

'I think you have enough Suave shoes, don't you?' I take the heels from him and place them back on the shelf. 'How many pairs has Lianna sent you this season?'

Aldo screws up his nose and shoots me a frown. 'Shirley, you can *never* have too many Suave shoes. Don't you know me at all?'

I hit him on the back playfully and let out a giggle. Almost immediately, an unpleasant twinge causes my stomach to flutter. My smile instantly falters and I feel guilty for allowing myself to laugh when just moments ago I was in the midst of a panic attack. Attempting to shake it off, I make all the right noises as Aldo grabs a basket and starts to load it up with a selection of shoes, boots and trainers. I watch his eyes glint as he spends half a second considering each purchase. Not bothering to look at the price tag, he simply checks the sizing and drops them into his basket. You can almost see the bursts of happiness above his head as he picks up each pair. After feeling so low, actual joy in progress is fascinating to see. As he moves on to the jewellery counter, I find myself wondering if I will ever feel like that again.

It would help if I knew what was wrong with me. The thing is, I'm afraid to find out. I also have this secret fear of being officially labelled as mentally ill. It's easier to tell myself this will pass and that I don't need any help, any pills or any kind of therapy.

'Shirley?' Aldo's voice pierces my thought bubble, causing me to snap back to reality. 'Red or blue?'

'Mmm...' I look down at the two bracelets he is holding out. 'Red.'

He looks at me in bewilderment. 'Really? Even though the jacket is green? That would totally clash!'

I bite my lip anxiously, not wanting to admit that I haven't got a clue what he is talking about.

'Have you even been listening to me?' Dropping the blue bracelet into his basket, he leads me into a quiet corner of the shop. 'Are you okay?'

'Yes!' I hiss, my heart starting to pound once more. 'I'm fine!'

'We both know you're not *fine*...' Aldo sighs and shakes his head. 'If you aren't up to this, you just have to say.'

Shaking off his concerns, I fake a laugh and ignore the voice in the back of my mind that is warning me I'm out of my depth.

'For the final time, Aldo, I'm fine...'

Chapter 16

'What do you want to do for dinner?'
Aldo asks, slipping his arm through mine as
we head to the taxi rank. 'We could have
Indian, or should we just drink our weight
in champagne?'

An entire afternoon of pretending not to
be afraid has left me emotionally drained
and as a result, my battery is running on
empty. Aldo's attempts at fixing me with
cupcakes and sparkly things has gone
down like a lead balloon. Food is the *last*
thing on my mind and as much as I hate to
admit it, so is Aldo. I can't keep up this act
anymore, all I want to do is cower beneath
my duvet and shut out the rest of the
world. My face is physically aching from
forcing my muscles into a smile. Each time
I curl up my lips, I feel myself falling
deeper and deeper into a hole that seems
impossible to crawl out of. Nothing is
working.

'I'm not really hungry...' I try to sound
convincing as I prepare to make my
escape. 'Besides, I have to check on my
mum's house. I'll grab something there.'

'Okay...' Holding out his arm for a taxi, Aldo nods and takes a puff of his cigarette. 'We can check on the house and pick up a pizza on the way home.'

My stomach flips and I try not to show how exasperated I am. 'Actually, I'd rather go alone...'

'No chance.' Aldo cuts me off abruptly and shakes his head. 'I'm coming with you, end of story.'

'But...'

'I said *no*, Shirley.' His tone is so sharp that I physically flinch. 'I told you last night. If you won't let me take you to a doctor, then I'm staying with you until I see you turn a corner. That means twenty-four hours a day, seven days a week.'

Tipping back my head, I curse myself for letting things get this out of hand. Why couldn't I just have kept it together? Why didn't I just dust myself down and carry on?

'I appreciate what you're trying to do here. I really, *really*, do.' I take his hands in mine and squeeze them gently. 'I'm feeling so much better already, but I still need a little breathing space.' I'm surprising myself with how well the lies are starting to slip off the tongue. 'You go and order food. I'll meet you back at the apartment. I'll only be an hour.' Digging around in my purse, I fish out some notes and shove them into his pocket.

He holds my gaze for a moment too long before finally shrugging his shoulders and stubbing out his cigarette. 'Fine, but if you're not back in an hour, I swear to God I will call the police.'

I manage to fake a laugh as a cab pulls up next to us. 'I won't be long.' Climbing into the car, I give him a quick wave as the taxi races off into the night.

Being able to drop my forced smile fills me with sadness as I realise this is who I really am now. My body sinks into the seats as the driver speeds along the country lane. I sway left and right with the movement of the car, closing my eyes to reveal the darkness that has become so comforting to me. I could cry with relief that I finally have a few moments alone to allow the emotions to come out.

Just as I am about to let the tears fall, the car comes to a stop outside my mother's house. Offering the driver my card to make the payment, I slide over the seat and slam the door shut. I didn't need to check on the place. The enormous gates and monitored alarm system provide the ultimate security, but knowing there's no one here appeals to me right now.

Not bothering to turn on the light, I step inside and look around the vacant hallway. Reaching for the bannister, I drag myself up the stairs and come to a stop in front of my mum's bedroom. Her familiar scent drifts out and I can almost feel it pulling me inside. Taking a seat on the edge of her bed, I bury my face into her feather pillow. Memories of my childhood come flooding back to me as I curl up into a little ball. Back then I felt safe and protected, in the way that only children can feel.

The walls of the dark room seem to close in on me, but this time I'm not scared. I want them to wrap their arms around me and protect me from this hideous feeling inside. From the outside world that gives me panic attacks and from the alarming idea that I may never return to my normal self.

I need a mother. Not *my* mother, but a mother who will hold me and tell me everything is going to be alright. I'm twenty-five, I'm an actual grown-up and here I am, crying into my mother's pillow and I don't even know why. I have the life that most people would kill for. Why can I no longer appreciate the good things around me? Why am I void of any feeling that isn't negative? Tears spill down my cheeks and I am powerless to stop them.

Not only am I sad about my past, but I am now petrified of the future. What happens next for me? I don't have a job, I can't afford to run the apartment by myself and apart from Aldo, I don't have a single real friend. I don't even know where to start with putting my life back together. It's like my future has been shattered into a million pieces. Some of those pieces are so broken I couldn't fix them if I tried. I feel like something inside is telling me this is where my story ends, this is it for me. The titles are about to roll and the curtain is getting ready to fall. Game over. Thank you for coming and goodnight.

My phone pings in my pocket and I know without looking that it will be Aldo checking up on me. I can't go back to the apartment and pretend I'm okay because that's what Aldo wants to hear. I just can't. I know I should tell him how I'm feeling, but the idea of what might happen if I reveal I want to close my eyes and never open them again is worse than keeping up this performance.

I can't carry on like this. I have to address it. I *need* to address it. If I don't, I am extremely worried about what might happen. What I might do to myself if this carries on for a moment longer. Ignoring my chirping phone, I wander around the dark room until I find myself in the en-suite. My head starts to throb as my brain goes into overdrive. *What? Why? When? How?* So many questions are running through my mind and each one has an awful answer. Flicking on the light, I scour the cabinets for some painkillers.

Finally locating a medicine box at the back of the towel cupboard, I perch on the edge of the bath and flip open the lid. A dozen bottles stare up at me as I select a strip of ibuprofen and grab a glass from the counter. Popping the pills into my mouth, I fill the cup with water and gulp them down. The cold liquid sends shivers down my spine as I bend down to fasten the box. Pausing with my fingers on the bottle of co-codamol, I decide to take one of those as well.

Sliding down onto the cold tiles, I run my fingers over the selection of tablets and study the labels. So many solutions for so many different ailments. You name the symptom and the answer is right here in this plastic container. Heartburn, indigestion, period cramps and diarrhoea. If only there was a single-dose pill to stop me from feeling like this. I am about to fasten the clip when I spot my mum's sleeping medication buried beneath a stash of plasters and antiseptic cream. Picking up the brown bottle, I turn the lid and listen to the click as I twist it repeatedly.

My mother has always had trouble sleeping. For as long as I can remember, she has popped a pill every night before crawling into bed. She's never mentioned why and I've never asked, but as soon as her head hits the pillow she is out like a light. Shaking the bottle, I push down on the cap and twist to release the child lock. I look down into the bottle and tip a single tablet into my hand. The tiny white pill seems to fascinate me as I run my eyes over the imprint. How can something so miniscule provide such a welcome escape from yourself? From your mind and your thoughts?

I hold the bottle up to the light and squint at the faded label. Two should do the trick. Two of these and I will be free until tomorrow. Free of emotion, free of feeling and free of the crippling anxiety I can physically feel weighing me down. Tipping out another tablet, I continue shaking the bottle until every last one is in the palm of my hand. My ears ring slightly as I jiggle around the pills. There must be around sixty here. Sixty chances to escape into nothingness.

Letting the empty bottle fall to the floor, I pass the tablets from one hand to the other. A tear slips down my cheek and I furiously bat it away. After months of keeping my emotions bottled up, I have finally tired of crying. I am sick of seeing myself with a tear-stained face and red eyes. Leaning over the bathtub, I refill the glass with water and pop a sleeping pill into my mouth. My skin buzzes as I feel it slip down my windpipe and into my stomach. A rush of adrenaline hits me and I immediately feel a wrench of hope.

I'm considering taking another one when my phone rings again in the bedroom. A sob escapes my lips as my chirpy ringtone drifts into the bathroom, echoing around the tiled room.

I look down at the mountain of pills in my palm and silently cry. The tiny voice in the back of my mind eggs me on, telling me that if I just take these I won't need to suffer anymore. I won't need to dread each day and lay awake each night. The awful churning inside me will stop. It will be like it never existed in the first place. I can go back to the person I was just a few months back. Everything will be erased. All the bad memories that are causing me to feel so horrendously low will be... *gone*.

I glance at my watch and realise that I have been staring at the tablets for the past fifteen minutes. Raising another tablet to my lips with a trembling hand, I quickly throw it back before I can change my mind. My eyelids start to become heavy and I realise that the first sleeping tablet I took is starting to take effect. Fighting against it, I hold on to the edge of the bath as I start to feel a little woozy. Struggling to keep my focus, I accidentally drop the remaining tablets on the floor.

There's a bang downstairs as I desperately scramble around on the tiles for the pills. Locating another two by the sink, I frantically try to pick them up as my eyes glaze over.

'Shirley?' Aldo's voice hits me like a rock as I realise that he's here.

Throwing myself at the door, I struggle with the lock as my legs give way beneath me.

'Shirley! You knew the rules! One fucking hour!' His footsteps become louder and I cover my ears to drown them out. 'Shirley, stop playing around. Where are you?'

I wrap my arms around my body and stare at the tablets in front of me.

'Go away! Just leave me alone…' My voice trails off into panic-stricken cries as I lie down on the tiles.

'Shirley! Open this door or I'm going to kick it down!' Aldo tries the handle one last time before proceeding to kick at the lock.

Realising this is the last chance I will get to go through with this, I struggle to get my eyes to focus and snatch as many pills from the floor as I can. Adrenaline surges through me as my body struggles to stay awake. Heaving repeatedly as I attempt to swallow the tablets, I manage to lean over the toilet bowl as vomit fires up my windpipe.

Resting my head on the seat, the sound of Aldo kicking down the door is the last thing I hear as a strange warmth takes over my body. Finally letting go, my entire life flashes through my mind's eye before everything falls into darkness...

Chapter 17

Slowly rolling onto my side, a searing pain fires through my temple as I attempt to lift my head off the pillow. Wincing in agony, I rub clumps of mascara from my dry eyes and breathe through the discomfort. The bed sheets stick to my sweaty skin as I realise I'm in my bedroom. The bitter taste in my mouth indicates that I have a hangover and the vomit in my tangled hair tells me it's a bad one.

Using whatever energy I have to sit up straight, my brow crumples as I notice Aldo curled up beneath the duvet next to me. My stomach churns and I clasp my hands to my mouth as vomit rises in my throat, before crashing back down into my stomach with a burn. Sensing my movement, Aldo sits bolt upright and lets out a gasp.

'What are you doing?' He shouts, his voice hoarse as he reaches out and grabs my forearm.

My headache intensifies and I hold my head in my hands. 'Can you not shout like that, please?'

Turning to face him, I frown when I realise he's fully dressed. I'm about to ask him why he's in my bed when a lightning bolt hits me. *The bathroom, the tears, the pills...* Mortification runs through my veins and my cheeks flush violently.

'How are you feeling?' He croaks, dark circles hanging beneath his eyes.

Licking my lips, every hair on my body stands on end as I rack my brains for something to say, anything at all to make light of the situation. What is the right answer here? How are you supposed to feel the morning after an attempted suicide?

'You really scared me last night...' Aldo lies perfectly straight and stares up at the ceiling.

Seemingly frozen to the spot, I keep my gaze fixed firmly on the floor.

'Did you want really want to... you know... do it.' He asks, his voice so low I can barely hear him.

Do it. It sounds so blasé, so innocent. Did I want to go to sleep and never wake up? Yes, of course I did. Did I want to take my own life by overdosing on super strength sleeping pills? I really don't know.

'Shirley, you're going to have to talk to me...' Aldo throws back the sheets and swings his legs over the edge of the bed.

'I don't know.' I manage, wrapping my arms around my knees. 'I honestly don't know what I was thinking...'

Pushing himself up, Aldo marches up and down the bedroom for what feels like an eternity before coming to a stop by the window.

'I've never been so scared in my entire life.' He has his back to me, so I can't see his face, but I can tell from the tone of his voice he is close to tears. 'I thought you had gone. I really did...'

'Aldo, I'm so sorry...' I stammer, looking down at the ground as he carries on talking.

'There were so many pills on the floor... You couldn't talk... You couldn't stand up...'

My heart pounds with shame and I try to hide behind my hair. 'I'm sorry. I didn't mean to scare you...'

'Then what the hell *did* you mean to do?' Aldo spins around and stares at me, his brow taught with fury. 'Go on, tell me. What did you think you were doing when you locked yourself in the bathroom and knocked back a handful of pills? How many did you even plan on taking? One bottle? Two?'

'I only took three pills. I swear it was only three...'

'You did just take three, I counted them, but only because I got there in time! Five minutes later and you probably wouldn't be here right now!' Anger seeps out of his every pore as he throws his arms in the air. 'How do you think that would have made me feel, Shirley? How would I have lived with myself if I would have found you dead in there?'

A lump forms in the back of my throat as I realise I wasn't thinking. In that moment, I didn't have a single thought for anyone else. My only concern was to end my own torment.

Aldo takes a deep breath and sits on the foot of the bed. 'I thought I could handle this myself. I thought I could fix whatever had gone wrong in your mind with champagne and shopping trips.' He runs his fingers through his hair and sighs sadly. 'You need help, Shirley. As in now, *today*. I'm making an emergency appointment with your doctor...'

My bottom lip starts to tremble and I give him a tiny nod in response. As much as I hate to admit it, he's right. I do need help. Whether I meant to leave this world or not isn't the issue anymore. The fact I even contemplated it is enough for me to acknowledge things are spiralling out of control. I have tried to pretend this isn't a big deal, that I can keep it to myself in the hope that it eventually goes away, but the truth is I *can't* fix myself. This is bigger than I or Aldo can deal with on our own.

'We can get through this, Shirley.' Aldo attempts a small smile and pulls me towards him. 'We might not have everything together right now, but together we can get through anything...'

* * *

The waiting room is just like I remember it, beige, clinical and full of sick people. Only this time, I am one of them. Aldo is right by my side, holding my quivering hand with a steely expression on his face. I don't quite believe this is *my* life that I am living. How did I end up here? You hear about people having episodes, don't you? You just never think it will happen to you.

A high-pitched ding pops my thought bubble and I look up to see my name emblazoned on the screen above. Aldo gives me a nod and I reluctantly stand to my feet. I feel the rest of the people in the room staring at me discreetly as Aldo leads me towards a door labelled *Surgery 3*.

'Everything's going to be okay...' Aldo whispers, clearly sensing my fear as he knocks on the dark, wooden door. 'Just tell her everything.'

'Everything...' I repeat, my blood running cold at the thought of telling a complete stranger my life story.

A muffled noise comes from inside as Aldo releases the handle and leads me into the tiny room. Stacks of papers surround a lady in a white coat, who is busily scribbling on a notepad. Motioning for us to sit down, she clacks at the keyboard and pushes a pair of glasses up the bridge of her nose.

'I shan't be a moment...' She presses a few more keys before folding her arms and turning to face us. 'How can I help you?'

Not being able to bring myself to say anything, the palms of my hands sweat profusely as I look down at my legs.

'Shirley...' Aldo brushes my hair out of my face as the doctor leans across the desk.

'I... I think I need some help.' I whisper, struggling to contain my tears. 'I've not been too well...'

'Okay...' The doctor slips her glasses into her blonde curls and frowns. 'Define *not well?*'

'I've just felt so low. I guess it started when my fiancé left me and I've gradually been feeling worse ever since. I tried to pick myself up and carry on, but each day just got harder and more difficult to get through...'

'Go on...' She presses gently, not taking her eyes off me.

I feel physically sick as I recall the past few weeks of my life. The tears that seem to be permanently running down my face make a return as I look at Aldo for help.

'She's had a bit of a rough time, aside from the breakup.' He explains, rubbing my back encouragingly. 'An establishment dropped her art work, then she discovered her biological father and started having panic attacks... It's been one blow after another.'

'And how does all that make you feel, Sadie?' The doctor's voice is calm and reassuring as she waits for me to respond.

'At first, I felt sad. I was angry and completely devastated.' I mumble, fidgeting with the cuff of my sleeve. 'Now I just feel, *nothing*. I'm not depressed, I'm afraid. I have this dread, this *fear* inside me that something terrible is going to happen.'

'What do think is going to happen?' The doctor exhales quietly and picks up a pen.

'I don't know. I really, really don't know. I just feel hopeless, like my life has no purpose. I feel empty and scared all the time. I have no interest in the things that I enjoy anymore. I can't eat. I can't sleep. I just want to stay in my bed. That's the only place I feel safe...'

'I'm very sorry to hear that.' The doctor smiles sympathetically and scribbles onto a notepad. 'Have you ever felt suicidal?'

I immediately look at Aldo and mentally beg him not to say anything. My heart sinks as he shakes his head and takes a deep breath.

'She took some pills last night...'

The doctor pauses with her pen in mid-flow and waits for him to elaborate.

'I didn't want to die.' I whisper, praying she realises I'm not suicidal. 'I just wanted to stop feeling like this. Even just for one night.'

She nods in response and bites her lip. 'How many pills did you take and what were they?'

'I took a couple of painkillers for a headache and then I spotted my mother's sleeping medication...' Bile rises in my throat as the memories come flooding back. 'I didn't take many, just three.'

'She was sick immediately after taking them.' Aldo adds, wrapping an arm around my hunched shoulders.

The doctor turns her attention to the computer and starts to type.

'I won't do it again. I promise I won't.' Tears stream down my face, creating a damp patch on my creased shirt. 'I just wanted a break...'

Clearing her throat, she looks at Aldo and places her hands face down on the desk. 'Could you give Sadie and I a moment alone, please?'

Aldo gives me a sideways glance and I hesitantly give him the nod to leave. Sliding out of his seat, he gives me a quick hug before heading to the door and disappearing back into the lobby.

'Okay, Sadie. I'm going to ask you some questions and I need you to answer them honestly...'

Climbing into the car, I feel weirdly numb as I look down at the pamphlets in my lap. After establishing that I wasn't a danger to myself, the doctor booked me an appointment to meet with a counsellor and sent me on my way. She did gloss over the various anti-depressant and anti-anxiety medications available, but we both agreed to try counselling before exploring other options. Between you and me, the idea of relying on a pill to trick my brain into thinking everything is alright makes my anxiety worse than it already is. Taking medication is like admitting that I do have something mentally wrong and the thought of that petrifies me.

One thing I have had to accept, is that the events of late have sent me into somewhat of a depression. The doctor used a whole variety of scary words, which I chose to block out, but her general diagnosis was that I am suffering from anxiety, depression and panic attacks. I wanted to yell at her that she was wrong and that I will be back to normal in a couple of days, but deep inside I know she is right. I just feel ashamed that I have let myself get this out of control over seemingly nothing. I feel weak, too fragile to cope with the things most other people shake off and move on from.

Letting out a sigh that makes my bones ache, I rub my face and try to loosen the knots in my tense shoulders. The sun is shining brightly onto the car and despite the clear skies, people are still walking around with thick coats and fluffy scarves. Resting my head on the window, I watch a family make their way towards the woods. A couple of dogs walk by their feet as a little boy runs ahead happily with his ball.

How are people just carrying on with their lives? How can they not know how horrendously low I felt last night? Regardless of what horrendous things happen to you, people might offer a few sympathetic words or an understanding cuddle, but they continue with their lives no matter what you're going through.

'Well, what did she say?' Aldo manages finally, fidgeting in his seat as he drums his fingers on the dashboard.

'Nothing, really.' I mumble, taking the leaflets and stuffing them into the glove compartment. 'She just asked me a bunch of questions and said somebody would be in touch about a counselling appointment.'

'And that's it?' He takes the information pack back out of the glove compartment and flips through the pages.

'Apparently so.' I turn away and look through the window. 'She also gave me a number to call if I feel like things are getting too much...'

When I walked into that surgery, I had a tiny glimmer of hope that I would be finally be cured. That the pretty doctor behind the big desk would take one look at me and tell me she had the exact remedy to take away the pain. Unfortunately, it seems anxiety and depression aren't as easy to fix as a headache or a nasty cough.

'Alright, if that's all we can do here let's get you home.' He starts up the engine and puts his foot on the accelerator when his phone starts to ring in his jacket pocket. Cursing under his breath, he pulls on the handbrake and opens the driver's door.

'Sorry about this...'

He slams the door shut and I watch him wander around the car as he talks into the handset. The radio is playing quietly, but I can still hear every word he is saying.

'I can't just *leave* her, Edward...'

'She needs me right now...'

'I don't know. A week, maybe, two...'

'This isn't about us. It's about friendship...'

'She doesn't have anyone else...'

'What the hell is the matter with you?'

'Well, maybe that's not a bad idea...'

Kicking up a pile of gravel, Aldo picks up a stone and throws it in frustration.

'Is everything okay?' I murmur, giving him a sideways glance as he jumps back into the car and pulls out into the stream of traffic.

'Everything's fine! Totally fine!' Aldo stammers as he indicates right and swings the car into the fast lane.

'You don't need to stay with me. If it's causing problems with you and Edward, please don't feel like you...'

'Edward isn't my concern at the moment, you are.' Aldo places a reassuring hand on my knee as we fire down the motorway. 'All I am interested in right now is getting you better.'

Guilt rushes through me as we continue on our journey home. As bad as I feel that Aldo is getting grief from Edward, if I didn't have him around, I would literally have no one. My mum is more interested in topping up her tan and as for my girlfriends, Piper made it clear she thinks I am pretty pathetic and Ivy is getting busy with my ex. I think it's safe to say they're not going to be the best support network.

We stop at a set of traffic lights and I glance at a bustling bar. Am I hungry? Thirsty? What am I supposed to do now? Until I get this appointment, I just don't know what I'm going to do with myself. The impending doom that has tormented me for weeks is still very much with me. It hasn't decided to subside just because I sat in front of a doctor for half an hour. Panic starts to buzz in my ears as I wonder what exactly awaits me in counselling.

'I don't want to go to counselling...' I whisper, unbuckling my seatbelt as we enter the gates to the apartment block.

Aldo doesn't answer, choosing to reply with a sad look instead. Following him into the building, I avoid the mirror as we step into the lift and ride up to our floor. This building has become like my prison. It's the only place in the world I feel like I'm allowed to be. Every time I leave I feel like I'm violating my probation. Like I am escaping my capture. A capture that I fear I'm beginning to become attached to.

I slide the key into the lock as Aldo buries his nose in the pamphlets I was given at the surgery. Noticing the words *mental illness*, *sectioning* and *psychotic* on the page he is reading, I excuse myself to take a shower and slip into the bathroom.

As I strip down to my bare skin, I repeat what the doctor said over and over in my mind. It's official, I'm mentally ill. Not only do I have to cope with panic attacks, I've now been diagnosed with having anxiety and depression, too.

I sit on the edge of the tub and watch the water fire out of the shower head. I've never really thought about the health of my mind before. I take vitamins, watch my weight and stay away from cigarettes, but there's no daily supplement on the shelves to keep mental illnesses at bay.

Dread washes over me as I realise I might have a long, hard road ahead. The doctor warned me that although help is available, the path back to mental wellness isn't always an easy ride. The question is, am I strong enough to survive the journey?

Roughly drying my hair with a towel, I quickly brush my teeth and wrap my dressing gown tightly around my body. The sun is starting to set in the sky, casting my usually bright and airy room in shadow. Dropping my towel into the laundry basket, I wander over to the balcony and throw open the doors. The evening air pinches against my wet skin as it whooshes around my body. Not being deterred, I lean over the balustrade and look down at the forest below. The trees have finally lost their leaves. One by one they have turned brown at the edges and gently floated to the ground. Like a snake shedding its skin, the trees just let go of parts of them they've carried for so long.

I find myself quietly transfixed on the scene, mesmerised by how much I can relate to it. Detaching myself from all the bad energy that has been weighing heavily on my mind and clouding my judgement is exactly what I need to do. Just accept the past and embrace the future. No fear, no anxiety, just let it go. If only it came as naturally as the seasons do. Out with the old and in with the new.

'What are you doing out here?' Aldo steps out onto the balcony and zips up his jacket. 'It's freezing.'

'I was just getting some air.' I turn to face him and take a seat in one of the rattan loungers. 'Don't worry, I wasn't going to throw myself over...'

He shoots me a glare and I immediately feel bad. 'Not funny, Shirley.'

'Sorry...' I mumble, pulling a cushion onto my lap. 'I was just trying to make light of the situation.'

Aldo doesn't respond and takes a pamphlet out of his pocket, quickly becoming engrossed in the text.

'This is bullshit.' He mutters under his breath, his brow creasing into a frown as he holds the page an inch from his face.

'What is?' Shuffling around in my seat, I cross my legs to get comfortable and turn my back to the breeze.

'It says here it can take weeks if not *months* to get a counselling appointment.'

He pulls out his phone and starts to tap at the screen.

A mixture of relief and fear rushes through me. On one hand, I am thankful for escaping the dreaded counselling for a while longer, but on the other, I'm scared of what might happen in the meantime.

'Hold on, look at this.' Aldo clears his throat and passes me the handset. 'There's an Anxiety Anonymous meeting in Wilmslow tomorrow night.'

'Wilmslow?' I repeat, my mouth becoming dry as butterflies flutter in my stomach.

'What's the problem with Wilmslow?' He asks, adjusting the waistband on his jeans and reaching for the ashtray. 'It's just around the corner.'

'*That's* the problem.' The hairs on my arms stand on end as I picture our neighbouring town. 'It's so close to home. Cheshire's a small place, people talk.'

'I don't think now is the time to be bothered about idle village gossip, do you?' Not accepting my protests, he stuffs the leaflets into his jacket and shrugs his shoulders. 'You're going tomorrow and I'm coming with you...'

How did it come to this? Blinking back tears, I tap my fingers on the dashboard and try to keep calm. All the way here I have wanted to pull on the handbrake and race back to the safety of the apartment. A part of me hates Aldo for making me do this, but inside I know running away from my problems isn't going to help me one iota.

'Can you *please* let me do this on my own?' I ask for the tenth time, struggling to stop my legs from trembling.

Shaking his head as we swing around a roundabout, Aldo changes gear and sighs. 'Nope.'

'Why not?' I retort, panic rising in my throat. 'Having you there to hold my hand makes me feel like a mental patient. It's bad enough I have to do this in the first place...'

Indicating left, a hurt expression washes over his face and I kick myself for snapping at him. 'I just want to support you through this, that's all.'

'I know and I can never thank you enough, but I really feel like I have to do this alone.' Noticing that we are getting close to the destination, I pull my handbag onto my knee and get ready to jump out. 'Can you trust me to do this one thing by myself?'

Aldo rubs his face wearily and stares straight ahead before reluctantly nodding. 'Fine, but I'm going to be right here waiting for you when you come out.'

'Thank you...' Genuinely touched by his faith in me, I try to keep my voice steady as we approach the building. 'I'll get out here. I just need to clear my head before I go inside.'

Coming to a sudden stop, Aldo unlocks the doors and gives me a quick hug. 'You've got this, Shirley. Just remember, everyone else in there is going through the same thing.'

Not daring to reply in case I burst into tears, I flash him a scared smile and jump out of the car. As usual, the street is super busy and I fight against the urge to run to the taxi rank as I make my way towards the support group. I must have walked along this very path a thousand times and not once have I given this building a second glance. With blinds in every window and clinical signs at the entrance, it almost looks like a library.

Shoppers push past me as I try to gather up the courage to go inside. What do I even say once I am in there? *My name is Sadie and I'm here because I tried to kill myself?*

'Sadie?' A high-pitched voice makes me jolt to attention. 'Is that you?'

Brushing my hair out of my face, I scan the crowd of people to pinpoint the voice.

'It *is* you!' This time, Zara's voice is unmistakable. 'What are you doing here?'

Coming to a stop in front of me, her eyes widen as she gives me a quick once-over. My pale skin and tired eyes make a stark contrast to Zara's scantily-clad outfit and I can tell from the expression on her face she's mortified by the state of my appearance.

Her eyes land on the sign behind my head, but before I have the chance to explain, Piper and Ivy step out of the beauty store behind her. Laughing and joking, they cackle loudly as they head over to us.

'Well, well, well! What do we have here?' Piper smacks her lips together and nudges me on the shoulder. 'I would ask if you're feeling better, but you look like the walking dead!'

The other two join in with her laughter as panic takes hold of my body. I knew coming here was a bad idea. We should have chosen one that was out of town, somewhere as far away as possible.

'We're going to Precious, do you want to come?' Piper rests a hand on her hip and taps her foot impatiently. 'Although you might want to go home and change first...'

'Piper, I think Sadie might already have plans...' Zara points to the discreet sign behind me and raises her eyebrows.

I feel my blood run cold as Piper and Ivy squint at the logo. The pair of them exchange puzzled glances, but I'm too transfixed on Ivy's jacket to care. I'd recognise that battered, leather jacket anywhere. I've worn that jacket. I've run my fingers over those Harley Davidson badges. Despite my efforts to stop it, my heart sinks to my feet. That jacket belonged to Spencer's father. Spencer didn't go anywhere without it. Catching me staring, Ivy immediately looks away guiltily and tries to hide the badges behind her handbag.

'Anxiety Anonymous?' Piper scoffs, rolling her heavily made-up eyes. 'Give me strength...'

I glance at the taxi rank and consider making an escape when the door to the support group opens.

'Are you joining us?' A mature lady asks, looking around the three of us and smiling. 'We're about to start.'

Piper, Zara and Ivy stare at me as I look between the grey-haired woman and the three girls I used to call my friends.

Not daring to look at Piper, I lift my handbag onto my shoulder and nod.

'Great, come on in.' She motions for me to follow her inside, leaving the girls mocking me on the side of the street. 'I'm Julia.'

Their heckling fades into silence as I am led through a dimly lit corridor. Julia's selection of bohemian bracelets jangle together as she walks, creating a loud clang against the eerily quiet background. The walls are covered in various posters, each one depicting a different mental illness and the phone numbers to call if you need help.

Pushing open the door to a room on the right-hand side of the lobby, she stands back for me to step inside. Unlike the hallway, this room is open and bright, with a circle of plastic chairs in the centre of the empty space. There's a desk adorned with biscuits behind the chairs, next to a sign that instructs you to help yourself. Around twenty people are gathered around a coffee machine, some whispering quietly, others sipping from their paper cups in silence.

Feeling incredibly uncomfortable, I look through the small window in the door and wonder if I can flee without anyone noticing.

'Okay, if you would like to choose a seat, we are about to begin.' The lady who invited me in pulls out a chair at the front of the circle as people follow suit and start to fill up the seats.

Forcing myself to put one foot in front of the other, I walk to the nearest chair and perch on the edge, just biding my time until I can make my escape.

'For those of you who are joining us for the first time, my name is Julia and I would like to welcome you to this Anxiety Anonymous meeting.' She casts a glance in my direction and I reply with a thin smile. 'Making the decision to walk through that door today is the first step on your journey back to mental wellness.'

I look around the circle and feel surprised by how many people are here. People from all walks of life and not a single one would you expect to be suffering from a mental health problem.

'This is a safe space, anything you say here is completely confidential. Whether it be anxiety, depression or simply stress, you're not alone in your struggles. Here at Anxiety Anonymous, we aim to guide one another through the hard times and celebrate the good.' Julia beams broadly and clasps her hands together in her lap. 'Now, does anyone have anything they would like to share with the group?'

I hold my breath as she looks around the room, before nodding at a man in a suit who has his hand in the air.

'I've had a pretty tough week.' Loosening his tie, he rubs his bald head and looks down at the ground sadly. 'I thought I finally had this under control, but these past few days have been difficult, to say the least.'

I can hear my heart beating as I listen to him speak, fascinated by how easily he's sharing these personal details.

'I've had to cancel meetings, miss appointments, skip my kid's school activities...' He trails off as Julia opens her mouth to speak.

'And why have you felt the need to do that, Alec?' Julia leans forward in her seat as the rest of us stare at him with bated breath.

'I just feel like I can't handle things at the moment.' Fiddling with his watch, he lowers his voice to a whisper. 'My wife's starting to tire of me and I don't blame her. At first, she was sympathetic, but now she's had enough. She doesn't understand how I can be okay one minute and unable to function the next.' Alec looks around the group and I can hear true sorrow in his voice. 'As soon as I allow myself to forget about the anxiety, it returns like a punch to the gut and then I feel like a fool for pretending it had gone in the first place. Can any of you relate to that?'

Yes, I think to myself. I can absolutely relate to that! He looks directly at me and I immediately look away. A chorus of agreement echoes around the room and I'm amazed that they're all agreeing, too.

'The first thing we all have to accept about anxiety, is that we are *never* going to be completely free of anxiety.' Julia's calming voice has me transfixed, but what she's saying is sending off alarm bells. 'Anxiety is part of the normal way in which your body operates. When anxiety strikes, you may feel like something terrible is going to happen, you may feel like you are losing control or that you are going to come into great harm. I can assure you that *none* of those things will happen.'

Julia pauses and looks at each one of us individually, her blue eyes swiftly moving from one to the next. 'Anxiety is a normal emotion, just like all the others. It only becomes a problem when we allow it to escalate beyond reason.' Stopping for breath, she turns her attention to a chair at the opposite end of the circle. 'Yes, Ruby?'

I strain my neck to see who she's talking to and notice a curvy teenager dressed in a quirky, black dress.

'If anxiety is a normal emotion, is depression normal too?' She cocks her head to one side as she speaks and screws up her little nose. 'Sometimes I feel like my levels of anxiety cause me to fall into a depression. The constant fear of panic attacks makes my life a living hell...'

My jaw drops open as Ruby continues to talk. I said those exact words to the doctor just yesterday. Half of me wants to laugh with joy. I'm not alone in this after all! A tear slips down Ruby's cheek as she recalls staying in her bed for days on end and I instantly regret finding a glimmer of hope in her misfortune. I know that gut-wrenching fear all too well. The one that makes you want to fall asleep and never wake-up again.

Ruby bats away the tears and I physically have to stop myself from diving out of my seat and giving her a hug. She can only be eighteen, nineteen at the most. Someone so young shouldn't have to deal with the torture that is anxiety, depression and panic attacks. She should be enjoying herself, dancing the night away with her friends and planning for her future. Not curled up in bed wishing the days away because she's too afraid to face the world.

Julia adjusts her glasses and exhales sharply. 'Unfortunately, anxiety and depression can sometimes roll into one vicious circle. The anxiety offsets the depression and vice versa. Although they both have a similar impact on us, anxiety and depression are quite different indeed and *can* be separated if we train the brain to change the way we think.'

You could hear a pin drop as the entire room falls into a captivated silence.

'You see, depression is generally connected to our feelings about *past* events and anxiety is associated with trepidation of the *future*. My aim in these meetings is to help you all to start living in the *present* where anxiety and depression simply cannot survive...'

The Trail in Her Wake

'I'd like to thank you all for coming along today. I really hope you've found this session beneficial.' Julia pushes out her chair and rests her hands on her hips. 'Please feel free to stay behind and chat amongst yourselves. I have to shoot off to another meeting in Hale, but I hope to see you all on Friday. Oh, and don't forget, there's always the forum if you find yourselves struggling in the meantime.'

A small round of applause rings around the group and I join in with the ovation. I'm so glad that Aldo talked me into this. In just one hour I feel better than I have in months. The doctor was right, jumping straight to medication isn't the answer here. I have learned so much about coping techniques, breathing exercises and maintaining a positive mental attitude in a single session. If I can feel this much better so quickly, how much progress can I make in the coming days and weeks?

Feeling super optimistic, I smile at Julia as she heads for the door. With a quick wave, she slips on her patchwork coat and disappears into the lobby. A few of the other people follow after her and I shove my hands in my pockets, wondering if I should join the others for a coffee. It feels a little strange, having a caffeine hit with people whose names I don't even know. Maybe I should just go...

'Would you like a drink?' A small voice asks, tapping me on the shoulder.

Spinning around, I smile as I see Ruby holding out a paper cup gingerly.

'Oh, thank you.' Accepting the cup from her, I take a sip and grimace at the taste. 'It's... *lovely*.'

'It's not the best.' Ruby laughs as blood rushes to her face. 'But it's all we have.'

'It's great!' I lie, looking down into the murky dishwater and wondering where I can dispose of it. 'Thank you so much.'

'Is this your first time?' Ruby asks, tucking her raven hair behind her ears. 'I haven't noticed you here before.'

'It is my first time.' I confirm, leaning against the wall. 'I didn't know what to expect, but I've found it really helpful.'

'Yeah, Julia's amazing.' Ruby sits on the edge of the desk and swings her legs back and forth. 'My parents get so frustrated with me. They don't understand why I can't *pull myself together*, but Julia just gets it.'

I nod along and take another sip of my drink. I can't imagine how difficult it must be to try and fight this at Ruby's age.

'How long have you been coming here?' I ask, discreetly disposing of the poor excuse for a coffee.

Ruby looks to the left and counts on her fingers. 'A year, maybe a year and a half.'

'*A year?*' I feel my mouth fall open at her response.

If she's been coming here for an entire year, why isn't she fixed? Why is she still plagued with anxiety?

'I know what you're thinking, but when I first started coming here I was so much worse than I am now. This place saved my life... *literally*.'

My heart drops and I try not to show my disappointment. Maybe this isn't the quick-fix I was hoping for. I suddenly feel a fool for allowing myself to believe I could cure myself with a few breathing techniques and the odd coping mechanism.

'There you are!' Hearing a familiar voice, I look up to see Aldo striding into the room. 'I saw everyone leave and panicked when you didn't come out.'

Guilt runs through me as I realise I've worried him. 'Sorry, I was just talking to Ruby.'

Aldo shifts his gaze to my new friend and holds out his hand for a polite shake. 'Hi, Ruby.'

'So, how was it?' He asks, turning his attention to me with a hopeful expression on his face.

'I'll leave you guys to it.' Ruby drains her coffee cup and jumps down from the desk. 'Hope to see you next week.'

'Definitely.' I call after her, as she grabs her coat and slips out into the lobby.

The door silently closes and Aldo tugs on my sleeve. 'She seems very nice.'

'She is nice.' I mumble quietly, keeping my eyes fixed on the door.

Aldo looks at me warily and holds out his arm for mine. 'How about we go grab some lunch and you can tell me all about it?'

The fear makes a comeback and I shake my head in response. 'I just want to go back home.'

Aldo's face falls as he realises that a single group counselling session isn't going to be enough to erase this torment.

'Okay... Well, let's grab some food and we can have a duvet day.' Linking his arm through mine, Aldo leads me down the lobby and back towards the car.

Despite my efforts to resist, I turn back and steal a glance at Precious. They'll be in there right now, sipping champagne and chuckling because silly Sadie can't cope with life. I picture them clinking together their glasses and cackling, their stomachs creasing with laughter at the very thought of me.

My chest becomes tight and I wonder how I have slipped straight back into the negative state of mind I was in before the meeting. When I was listening to Julia, I felt hopeful and optimistic that this was the answer. As soon as I've stepped back out into the world, I am right back where I started. Ruby's words ring around my mind and try to block them out. She has been going there for a year. Three hundred and sixty-five days, yet she's *still* suffering.

'Shirley?' Aldo repeats, pointing to the fast food sign above his head. 'What do you want?'

I stare at his face and realise I haven't been listening. 'Anything.' I mutter, knowing that whatever he gets for me I won't eat anyway.

The wind blows my hair into my face as Aldo beeps open the car and heads into the eatery. Climbing into my seat, I recall Julia mentioning a forum and load up the internet on my phone. I find it almost immediately and don't hesitate in pressing the *register* key. After tapping out my email address and phone number, the form instructs me to pick a username. Typing out my name, I frown at the screen as it tells me the username I have chosen is already taken. I try adding various digits and let out a frustrated sigh as I'm informed they're all taken as well.

Turning to stare out of the window, I look up and down the street until my eyes land on the sign outside the Anxiety Anonymous building. Going back to the website, I stretch out my fingers and jab at the keyboard.

Congratulations!
Anxiety Girl is available!

I smile in satisfaction at my phone as Aldo pulls open the driver's door and tosses me a paper bag. 'They didn't have much left, so I just got a couple of sandwiches.'

Immediately putting the car into gear, he flicks on the radio and puts his foot down.

'Thank you.' I mumble, taking a quick look in the bag and stashing it at my feet. 'Where are we going?' I add, realising we're heading in the opposite direction to home.

'Just taking a quick detour...' Turning onto a country lane, he taps his fingers on the steering wheel.

My stomach cramps as the prospect of another panic attack hits me. 'Aldo, I *really* want to go home...'

'I know you do, but while you were in the counselling session I did a little research.' He smiles confidently at me and I resist the urge to open the door and throw myself out onto the busy road. 'Giving into the anxiety is the worst thing you can do. All the sites I visited advised the same thing, you need to acknowledge the anxiety is there and carry on as normal.'

The word *normal* makes my skin sting with fear. But I'm not normal, I feel so far away from normal that I'm beginning to forget what normal is. Before I can protest further, Aldo brings the car to a smooth stop and turns down the radio. Forcing myself to look up, I feel my lips stretch into a smile. This is our spot. This is where we come to when the sun is shining and we want to drink wine in the shade of the many rustling trees.

'Eat...' Aldo instructs, passing me a cheese sandwich and a packet of crisps.

'Thank you for making me go to the meeting...' Slowly opening the box, I pick at the bread half-heartedly. 'I'm so glad I went.'

Aldo's face breaks into a smile as he bites into his lunch. 'That's fantastic! What happened? Tell me everything!'

'It was exactly like you would imagine a support group to be. There was a circle of chairs, people took it in turns to speak about how they were feeling...'

Aldo nods enthusiastically and wipes his hands on his jeans. 'Did you talk about what you've been going through?'

I shake my head and open the packet of crisps. 'Not this time. I was weirded out just being there. I was listening to the others speak about their troubles and I kept asking myself, *how did I end up here?*'

'How do you think you ended up here?' Aldo asks, immediately regretting the question escaping his lips. 'Sorry for asking, it's just that the websites I was reading said it was good to talk about it.'

Popping a couple of crisps into my mouth, I subconsciously rub my finger tattoo. 'I honestly don't know...'

Aldo nods and dives into the crisp packet. 'When did you first start to feel, you know, *down*. I know this all started with Spencer, but when did you realise you were losing control?'

A flurry of different emotions rush through my body as I am mentally transported back through the last couple of months.

'When things ended with Spencer I felt weirdly numb. It was like I just carried on with my life. I surprised myself with how well I coped, but as the days turned into weeks, I started to fade away inside. When I realised dating other men wasn't making me feel any better, I got this sinking feeling that just wouldn't go away.'

Aldo abandons his food and motions for me to continue.

'I tried talking to the girls, but you know what they're like. They thought I just needed to get over it. And I tried to get over it, I really did. My plan to move on from Spencer was to throw myself into my work, but then that was taken away from me, too.'

My voice starts to wobble and I fake a cough to cover it.

'I'm so happy for you and Edward, I really am, but when you announced you were moving out, it broke my heart a little bit. We've become so close these past few years, you're like a brother to me.'

I notice Aldo's eyes glass over and curse myself for telling him how I really feel.

'As hard as I found losing Spencer, Precious and you to Edward, the thing that hurt the most was finding my dad. I don't even know why. Just seeing him with this new life was like a blow to the stomach. It was a life that seemed so mundane and perfect when mine was falling apart. I've never been close to my mum, you know that, but I always had this secret fantasy of finding my father and being welcomed into a loving family. It turns out that my fantasy was exactly that, a fantasy.'

Feeling the tension lift from my shoulders, my chest heaves as I allow myself to cry.

'This is *good*, Shirley.' Aldo unbuckles his seatbelt and wraps his arms around me. 'This is all really, really good.'

'It is?' I manage, struggling to compose myself.

'Yes! You don't need to keep everything bottled up all the time. It's okay to be upset.'

Sniffing loudly, I take a napkin and wipe my tear-stained face.

'Do you realise this is the first time you've spoken to me about any of this? I knew you were struggling, but not once did you admit to me you felt so... *alone*.' Aldo wipes a smudge of makeup from my cheek and squeezes me tightly. 'Not talking about your feelings is like a red flag to a bull with depression and anxiety. Did you speak to anyone else about this?'

I shake my head and turn to look out of the window. 'I thought if I just ignored it and carried on, eventually, it would go away.'

Seemingly deep in thought, Aldo bites his lip before fixing his face into a smile. 'Well, there's two things I want to say. Firstly, I'm sorry you felt like you couldn't talk to me and secondly, I want you to promise me that you'll always come to me in the future.' I nod in agreement and rest my head on his shoulder. 'Together, we can get you out of this hole just as quickly as you fell into it.'

'Thank you...' I whisper, picking up my phone as an email pops up on the screen.

'Who's that from?' Aldo asks, squinting at the handset.

'Anxiety Anonymous has a forum for members to chat amongst themselves between sessions.' I pass him the phone and twist my hair into a messy ponytail.

'Anxiety Girl?' He smiles and takes a glug from the water he picked up earlier. 'Was Shirley Valentine not available?'

I playfully punch him on the arm and manage a small laugh. Feeling a genuine smile on my face is something I haven't experienced in such a long time. Promising myself to never take any glimpse of happiness for granted ever again, I take a deep breath and spit out the words I've been wanting to say all morning.

'I saw Ivy.' I blurt out, just as he puts his foot on the accelerator. 'She had Spencer's jacket on...'

Aldo looks like a rabbit caught in the headlights and I know immediately that something is awry.

'What is it?' I ask, already knowing I don't want to hear what he is going to say.

'Alright, I didn't want to say anything as I was worried how you would react.' He bites his thumb nail nervously and pulls on the handbrake. 'When you first mentioned that they were talking, I did a little investigating and word on the grapevine is that they've been dating for a *long* while. Some people are even saying it started before you guys... you know.'

Hearing my suspicions confirmed makes me feel strangely vindicated. Now it makes sense. It *all* makes sense!

'I also spoke to one of his ex-girlfriends on Facebook, he cheated on her as well. It seems that Spencer Carter has quite the history of promising the world to women and then dropping them.' Aldo steals a glance at me and rubs his temples. 'How did we get him so wrong?'

His words ring around my mind as I wait for the sadness to hit me, only it doesn't come. The only thing I feel is relief. No wonder we didn't make it! For the past couple of months, I've been trying to work out the reason behind Spencer's actions. I was torturing myself for ruining the only meaningful relationship I've ever had, but it turns out it wasn't my fault. It was him. It was *all* him. I almost want to laugh. If it wasn't Ivy, it would have been someone else. Another girl, another day, another affair.

'Are you okay?' Aldo asks cautiously. 'Please don't freak out...'

Inhaling sharply, I breathe out the tension that has been bothering me for so long. 'You have no idea how good it feels to hear that...'

'Good?' He repeats, narrowing his eyes at me suspiciously. 'Why?'

'Because now I can stop blaming myself!' I exclaim, throwing my arms in the air. 'I can finally stop replaying the whole relationship in my mind and wondering where it went wrong. It's like I finally have closure. I can finally start to accept that it wasn't meant to be and move on.'

Aldo opens and closes his mouth repeatedly, seemingly lost for words. 'Wow, I wasn't expecting you to take it so well. What a great way to look at it...'

'It's the *only* way to look at it.' I say sternly, remembering what we learned at the support group. 'Julia spoke a lot about finding the root cause of our problems, addressing them and moving on. Now I know the cause, I can start to put Spencer behind me. I feel better already. This is exactly what I needed. Julia was totally right. Julia's a genius!'

'That's fantastic advice.' Aldo breathes, giving me a high five. 'I just have one question... *Who the fuck is Julia?*'

Chapter 21

I have been staring at this screen for five solid hours. I just can't tear myself away. There must be hundreds of people on this forum, each one openly discussing their anxiety and depression with other users. Unbeknown to me, Anxiety Anonymous has branches all over the country. From London to Newcastle, members of the group are logging on day and night. I can't believe how many other people have been struggling with the exact same symptoms that I have. Some for years, some for just a few days, there's even a couple who are simply concerned about someone close to them.

I haven't posted a message yet or replied to a thread, but just knowing I am not alone brings me great comfort. I'm also realising there are people out there making my symptoms look like a drop in the ocean. Just reading the various stories is making me want to reach out and reassure them all they'll be okay. I hold my finger over a thread entitled *Coping Strategies* and double tap. I have already read this, but I've found it so useful that I want to read it over and over again.

It's like I've found this whole new world to disappear into. So far, I have downloaded calming apps, bought three self-help ebooks and signed up for email alerts on a dozen different blogs. The distraction of reading about others has taken my mind off my own troubles, but the second I remember I also have anxiety, my heart sinks and I'm right back where I started.

Pulling the duvet up to my chin, I flick off the light and grab my earphones from the bedside table. Thankfully, Aldo fell asleep on the couch not long after we arrived back at the apartment. I considered waking him, but he looked so content that I decided to cover him with a blanket and leave him to sleep. I'll never forgive myself for making this his problem. No matter how much he tries to convince me that anxiety isn't something you have any control over, the tapes I've been listening to tell me otherwise.

Loading up one of the apps on my phone, I hit *play* and fluff up my pillow. Gentle spa music floods into my ears as a soothing voice starts to speak.

Welcome to this thirty-minute meditation on anxiety management.
In this session, I am going to help you to realise that anxiety is not something you need to be afraid of. Once you discover how to manage your anxiety, you will learn to see each anxiety attack as an opportunity to show yourself just how strong you really are.

My brow furrows in confusion. I can't ever imagine being able to see anxiety as an opportunity. The thought of another panic attack makes me want to jump out of my bedroom window.

You're probably feeling quite sceptical right now.
You are right to feel this way.
Before we go any further, let's look at what anxiety really is.
Anxiety is the feeling of panic and fear, both of these are essential emotions.
Without panic and fear, we would not know how and when to protect ourselves from the dangers around us.

Running my legs over the sheets, I look up at the ceiling as the calming voice talks me into a slightly hypnotic state.

I am going to teach you how to keep your anxiety at a reasonable and rational level. Once you have learned to do this, you will be free from the crippling fear that has been casting a shadow over your life.

Allowing my eyes to close, I start to wonder where anxiety stops and depression begins. Which triggers the other or are they both so similar that they only differ in name?

Now we have established what anxiety is, I want you to think about what exactly anxiety does to you?
Cast your mind back to the first time you had an attack of anxiety?
Did your chest become tight? Did your head pound? Did you sweat profusely and have an all-encompassing fear running through your body?

I nod along to the tape and try to ignore my increasing heart rate. Just thinking about that dreadful day makes me nauseated.

If you answered yes to one or all of those questions, I want you to ask yourself what happened afterwards. No matter how terrible the anxiety made you feel, as soon as it passed you returned to feeling relatively normal. The unpleasant effects subsided and you were safe.

A frisson of annoyance hits me as I realise she's right. A part of me doesn't want to think of it like that. Like it is something so futile that it can be simply brushed off and moved on from. Those panic attacks were the most frightening and terrifying things to ever happen to me and I want them to be acknowledged as such.

Panic attacks cannot and will not hurt you. They may make you feel like you're having a heart attack or that something dreadful is going to happen, but I promise that no harm will come to you.
Panic attacks are the result of nothing more than adrenaline. This overproduction

of adrenaline is caused by our flight or fight senses.
These senses kick in when we become scared, frightened or intimidated.

Adrenaline? That thing people crave when they jump out of planes and buckle themselves into rollercoasters?

A little adrenaline can make us feel wonderful, but too much has quite the opposite effect, as you have unfortunately experienced.
But fear not, as with just a few simple techniques, we can retrain our bodies to understand exactly what is frightening and what is not.

This strangely resonates with me. There isn't anything scary about being sat in a waiting room, so why does the idea of it suddenly bring me out in hives? Why does even leaving my front door make me feel so apprehensive that I would rather stay inside? I never used to feel like this. So, what's changed?

More than likely, you will be able to think back to a time where anxiety didn't control you.

*A time where you didn't have this unnecessary fear making you so afraid. None of us are born with an anxiety disorder. Anxiety is an example of a learned behaviour and just as quickly as your body learned to react in this way, you can train it to **stop**...*

Chapter 22

'Are you sure you will be okay today?' Aldo asks, jumping down from the kitchen island. 'I would cancel my appointments, but Bella Lake is booked in and...'

'*Aldo!* It's fine.' I toss him his leather jacket and flash him the thumbs-up sign. 'I will be fine. I promise.'

He looks at me uncertainly and slips his cigarettes into his back pocket. 'Any news from the doctor?'

'They called with a counselling appointment for the week after next.' I reach into my handbag and grab my lip butter. 'In the meantime, I have Anxiety Anonymous. Don't worry.'

'So, what's on the agenda? Are you going to the support group today?' Aldo hovers by the door and fluffs up his ponytail.

'The next meeting is Friday.' I say sadly, wishing the time away until the next meet up. 'The app I was listening to last night advised to continue with your normal daily routine, even if it is the last thing that you want to do. So, I'm going shopping.'

'Shopping?' He repeats uneasily. 'Are you sure you're up to that?'

'If it gets too much, I will come straight back home.' I shoot him what I hope is a reassuring smile and usher him out of the door.

'You sound like you're about to walk the plank.' He observes, toying with his lighter. 'Don't push yourself too hard, too soon.'

'There's not a single part of me that *wants* to do this.' I confess, genuinely saddened that he has seen through my strong front. 'The thought of leaving the apartment makes my legs feel weak, but I want to beat this and I'm not going to do it by locking myself in my bedroom.' Not wanting to get emotional again, I grab my coat from the rack and reach for my trainers. 'Can you just go now, please?'

'Fine! I'm going!' Aldo lets out a laugh and flashes me a wink. 'You know where I'll be if you need me...'

The door closes behind him and I'm left alone with my thoughts. Knowing I will lose my nerve if I give myself time to overthink things, I watch Aldo's car pull out of the car park before following in his footsteps. Acting normal when you're so empty inside is quite a strange feeling. It's like eating when you've lost your appetite. It just seems… *wrong*. Doubts creep into my mind as I head towards the shops and I anxiously search my handbag for my earphones.

The second the now familiar spa music hits my ears, I feel instant relief. The app understands me, it knows exactly what I'm feeling. Just like Julia at Anxiety Anonymous, the app makes me feel safe and strong instead of scared and weak.

I listen to the app for the entire thirty minutes it takes for me to get to Wilmslow and remark at how much better I feel than when I left the house earlier.

Stepping into a department store, I pull out my earphones and scour the rails of clothes. With the shop being practically empty, the eager sales assistant doesn't waste any time in making her move.

'Are you looking for anything in particular?' She asks, stepping out from behind the counter and sashaying down the aisle.

'I'm just browsing, thank you.' Not being in the right frame of mind to make small talk, I turn to check out a stand of handbags.

Clearly sensing the tone, she quickly retreats to the till and picks up a nail file.

Running my fingers over the selection of pretty garments, a pair of boots catch my attention and I wander over to the display. Taking in the label, my heart freezes as I read the brand. *Suave.* The last time I was looking at a pair of Suave shoes I went to my mum's house and...

My ears start to ring as my stomach flips like crazy. I close my eyes and count as I pant, horrified at the thought of another panic attack. Remembering the breathing exercises recommended on the forum, I practice inhaling deeply and hold it for a few seconds before exhaling through my mouth.

Once confident the panic is subsiding, I bite my lip to stop it from trembling and pull open the door to the street. The little voice in the back of my mind tells me this was a test. It was a taster of what's to come if I don't turn on my heels and run back home. Shoving my hands into my pockets, I gingerly put one foot in front of the other and peer into the window of a perfume shop. The array of glistening bottles twinkle back at me, teasing me inside with their glitzy packaging.

The old me would be in her element right now. She would revel in covering herself with various scents and splash out on more bottles than she could use in a lifetime. Pressing my nose against the glass, I will myself to find that girl again. She must be in there somewhere, she *has* to be. I force the muscles in my face to smile, but my lips immediately fall flat. It's just not there. Not even a tiny part of me wants to go inside. I spot my mum's go-to perfume and my heart aches. She's probably wearing that right now as she lies in the sunshine with a cocktail. My heart hurts as I realise she hasn't even contacted me. Even after Aldo's phone call, her only concern was her precious mansion.

Moving my gaze along the display, I stop at Spencer's aftershave and laugh ironically as I spot Ivy's sickly scent sat next to it. Same brand, same bottle, just a different name. I find myself captivated by how well the two bottles fit together. It's almost as though they've been designed that way. Intentionally made to slot beside one another on the dressing table of a stunningly beautiful couple. Looking at my own perfume of choice, I realise Spencer's aftershave would never fit next to mine as seamlessly. My bottle is smooth, curved and delicately embossed, whereas his is angular and cubic, with more sharp edges than necessary.

Raindrops start to fall from the sky and I find myself questioning my sanity. What am I doing here? Why on earth am I torturing myself over bloody perfume bottles? I should just go back home. This whole mission was pointless. I don't feel better for carrying on as normal. If anything, I feel worse than I did this morning.

Deciding to flag down a taxi, I pull up my hood and make my way across the crowded street. The rain suddenly becomes heavy and I run under a café canopy to shield myself from the harsh conditions. It's like the weather knows how I am feeling. Nothing tells you that you should have stayed in bed like being caught in near hurricane conditions. A flurry of people brush past me into the restaurant and the delicious smell of freshly baked pastries drifts out onto the street.

Peering inside, I cup my hands around my eyes for a better view. The busy eatery is filled with wet people, each one warming their hands with the help of a coffee or a hot chocolate. The words of the lady on the app come rushing back to me and I wonder if I should join them.

No matter how terrible your anxiety makes you feel, no harm will come to you if you find the strength to push through it.

Reaching for the handle, I inhale sharply as I recognise a face at the back of the café. Neatly folding a newspaper, Ruby wipes her hands on a napkin before picking up a menu. I consider asking to sit with her when something stops me. Maybe it would be inappropriate. Isn't that the whole point of Anxiety Anonymous, that no one knows you attend the meeting outside of the group?

Convincing myself to walk away, I'm about to leave when Ruby lifts her head and looks directly at me. Slowly raising her hand, she smiles and gives me a wave. Instinctively waving back, I feel my heart start to race as she beckons me inside. The sound of coffee machines being fired up fills the air as I weave through the tables, incredibly nervous about what I should say. This girl is one of the only people in the world who knows what I'm going through and not only that, she is going through the same thing herself. It's like we have a secret, a sad secret, but a secret nonetheless.

'Hi...' I say cautiously, coming to a stop at her table. 'How are you?'

'I'm good...' She narrows her eyes and I remember that I haven't told her my name.

'Sadie.' I fill in for her, slightly embarrassed that a teenager has more manners than I do. 'Sadie Valentine.'

'Cool name!' Ruby smiles back at me and pulls out the chair next to her. 'Are you eating?' She asks, handing over a laminated menu.

Taking this as my cue to sit down, I remove my scarf and perch on the edge of the seat. 'I think I'll just get a coffee. I'm not that hungry today.'

'Anxiety rearing its ugly head?' She asks knowingly, twirling a beaded bracelet around her wrist. 'You should eat through it. Every time you let anxiety stop you from doing something that you would usually do, you're feeding it.'

'Feeding it?' I repeat, as an image of a dark creature tucking into a hamburger pops into my mind.

'You're making it stronger, more powerful. Think of anxiety as an actual person, like a living thing that you can name.' Ruby leans forward in her seat and lowers her voice to a whisper. 'Mine's Frank.'

'Frank?' I repeat, trying hard not to laugh. 'Why Frank?'

'I don't know...' She giggles and runs her fingers through her hair. 'Giving it a name makes it easier to keep under control. I mean, you can't reason with nothingness, can you? Since naming it, whenever I feel a panic attack coming on or I have a bad day, I talk to it.'

'You *talk* to it?' I gasp, completely bewildered.

Not being fazed by my reaction, Ruby nods in response. 'If my anxiety makes me feel like I don't want to get out of bed in the morning, I'm like... *Not today, Frank. Not today.* You should name yours, too. Let's call it... Ann.'

I let out a snort as a waitress walks past and shoots us a funny look.

'You think I'm crazy, don't you?' Ruby laughs and drums her fingers on the table. 'But then again you do attend the meetings, so I'm going to take a stab in the dark and say we're all mad here.'

I laugh along with her, but I can't help feeling a little confused at how different she seems today. At the Anxiety Anonymous meeting, she seemed so fragile, so afraid and so downtrodden. This girl sat in front of me seems like a different person entirely. I guess dealing with anxiety really is like a rollercoaster ride. One day you're up, the next you're down.

'You're staring at me...' Ruby whispers, trailing off as a waitress stops by our table. 'I'll have a double fudge hot chocolate with whipped cream and extra marshmallows.' She passes the waitress the menu and looks at me expectantly.

'I'll take the same.' I mumble, instantly regretting it.

With a quick scribble on her pad, the waitress removes our cutlery and dashes off to another table.

'So, why were you staring at me?' Ruby demands, puckering her lips as she waits for me to answer. 'My lip ring hasn't come out, has it?'

'No, your lip ring is fine.' I stammer, kicking myself under the table. 'I was just thinking how much happier you seem today...'

Ruby's face falls and she raises her eyebrows. 'Well, today is a good day. Yesterday was a different story entirely...'

'Do you normally have ups and downs?' The words are out of my mouth before I can stop them and I immediately worry I've overstepped the mark.

'Thankfully, I have more good days than bad, but I'm beginning to realise I will never be completely free of my anxiety.' She twists a strand of her hair around her finger and looks lost in thought. 'How long have you been a sufferer?'

'Not that long. A couple of months, maybe?'

Ruby widens her eyes and rests her elbows on the table. 'So, this is all new to you?'

'I guess it is, yes.' I am about to change the subject when a thought hits me. 'What about you? How long have you been a sufferer?'

Exhaling loudly, Ruby looks around the room and shrugs. 'I don't think there was a certain point where it started. I just think this is who I am. Even as a little girl I was such a worrywart. I would get myself into a right state about homework and my parents arguing. Even being a few minutes late for school would send me into a blind panic.'

I offer her a sad smile and look down at my tattoo. I feel like such a charlatan. Ruby has struggled with anxiety all her life and I'm piggybacking on her same symptoms because of little more than a breakup.

'There are no rules with anxiety. Some suffer continuously and others are hit with random bouts.' Ruby crosses her legs and wipes a few crumbs from the table. 'Just because you caught a cold last week, doesn't mean you won't catch another tomorrow.'

'You seem very open to talking about this.' I muse, becoming completely engrossed in the conversion. 'To be honest, I feel a little embarrassed.'

'Why?' She retorts immediately. 'Would you be embarrassed about a headache or a broken leg?'

'No?' I whisper, a little taken aback by her reaction.

She gives me a look that makes me want to giggle as the waitress returns with two ginormous glasses. With chocolate flakes sticking out of the top and pink marshmallows resting on the mountain of cream, they look more like a challenge than a drink.

'Enjoy!' The waitress hands us a couple of dessert spoons and scuttles into the kitchen.

Weighing up the huge glass in front of me, I twirl around the spoon and wonder where to start. Clearly not having the same struggle, Ruby plucks a flake with her fingers and scoops up a dollop of cream.

'If you don't eat that, it's one-nil to Ann.' She motions to the spoon in my hand and polishes off the flake. 'Are you a winner or a loser?'

'I don't really know *who* I am anymore...'

'Yes, you do. You're Sadie Valentine. You're the same person you've always been, you're just having a blip.' Ruby shoves some marshmallows into her mouth and reaches for a napkin.

Smiling back at her, I reluctantly dive into the cloud of cream. Due to the fact I haven't eaten properly in such a long time, my stomach has shrunk to the size of a pea and eating anything at all is a mammoth effort.

'Do you use the Anxiety Anonymous forum?' I ask, licking a spot of cream from my lip. 'I've found it really beneficial.'

Ruby nods and puts down her spoon. 'I do and it helps me a lot, but when I'm having a really bad day, *nothing* will drag me out of it. I just have to tell myself, this too shall pass. Those four little words have helped me more than you will ever know.'

I repeat the phrase in my head and feel a prong of hope. *This too shall pass.*

'Everything has to come to an end. That's just life.' Ruby points at my chocolate flake and grins. 'Are you eating that?'

Shaking my head, I offer her the flake and pour myself a glass of water from the jug on the table. 'Have you tried any other treatments for your anxiety?'

'Like what?' She asks, dipping the flake into her mug and taking a bite. 'Medication?'

I give her a nod and adjust the strap on my watch. 'Please tell me if my questions are inappropriate. I completely understand if you don't want to talk about it.'

'Talking is good.' Ruby's phone pings and she gives it a quick glance before dropping it into her handbag.

'People keep telling me that...' I mumble, remembering my conversation with Aldo.

'And you don't believe them?'

I shake my head and sigh. 'Talking about it seems to make it real and I don't want it to be real.'

'But it *is* real!' Ruby exclaims, finally abandoning her hot chocolate. 'Just because you can't see it doesn't mean it isn't there.' She pauses for breath and rests her elbows on the table. 'Try it. Come on, talk to me.'

I squirm in my seat and try to think of an excuse to leave. Having just been through this with Aldo, I really don't want to relive it again.

'Trust me...' Ruby places her hand on my arm and I know I can't refuse.

'I honestly don't know what to say. My relationship ended and things just seemed to get worse from there.' Ruby doesn't breathe a word, so I carry on talking. 'Some days I feel frightened and sad, others I'm just empty. It's like nothing matters to me anymore. I just want to hide away and be alone.' I look down at the table and shrug my shoulders. 'I guess the reluctance to leave the house is more down to the panic attacks than anything else.

I've never experienced anything quite like it. The thought of it happening again is just petrifying. Attending the meeting yesterday made me realise I'm not alone, but learning you're still struggling after a year of sessions makes me feel apprehensive. I guess kicking this thing is going to be more of a marathon than a sprint...'

I trail off as I realise Ruby is smiling manically at me.

'Do you even realise you've just answered *all* of your questions yourself?' Her eyes glisten as she clasps her hands together proudly.

'There's no shame in being vocal about your feelings, Sadie, and there's no shame in being afraid...'

Chapter 23

'I'm not doing it.' Aldo shakes his head and puffs on his cigarette. 'Sorry, but it's not going to happen.'

'Why not? You've been itching to get your hands on my hair for years.' I beg, following him around the balcony like a lost puppy. 'Please?'

'Nope.' He stretches out on one of the loungers and grabs the ashtray.

'Oh, come on!' Not willing to give up so easily, I take a seat next to him and rest my head on his shoulder. 'You're a bloody hairdresser and you're *refusing* to cut my hair!'

Blowing smoke rings into the air, Aldo chooses to ignore me completely.

'Fine. If you won't do it, I shall do it myself.' Jumping to my feet, I march across the balcony and throw open the doors. 'What do you recommend I use, kitchen scissors or textile shears?'

'For God's sake!' Aldo yells, stubbing out his cigarette and swearing under his breath. 'Just wait a minute!'

Stopping in my tracks, I hover my hand over the stand of utensils.

'If you're sure this is what you want, I'll do it.' He says hesitantly, taking the scissors and placing them out of my reach. 'I just don't want you to regret It when you're feeling better.'

'I *am* feeling better.' I exclaim, jumping up and down on the spot excitedly. 'I wouldn't ask if I wasn't a hundred percent sure it was what I wanted.'

Reluctantly nodding, Aldo exhales loudly and signals for me to calm down. 'Just tell me why it has to be right now. Why can't you sleep on it and see how you feel tomorrow?'

Pulling out my bobble, I let my hair fall around my shoulders. 'It just represents a time where I was so unhappy. I feel like I'm about to embrace a new chapter in my life and this seems the perfect way of marking it.'

Aldo looks at me uncertainly and frowns. 'I get that, I totally get it. My concern is that you're going to relapse and regret it. It would take ten years to get that length back. It wasn't long ago that you were rock bottom, who knows how you're going to feel tomorrow?'

Butterflies flutter in my stomach and I have to admit he has got a point. 'No one knows what tomorrow holds. I guess you'll just have to trust me on this.'

Rubbing his temples, Aldo doesn't say a word as he grabs his work bag from the front door. My heart pounds as he pulls out a cape and motions to the kitchen. A rush of adrenaline runs through me as I take a chair from the dining table and place it in the centre of the tiles.

Fastening the cape, Aldo wets my hair and carefully brushes out every last knot before picking up a pair of scissors. My skin prickles as he gently pushes down my head and makes the first snip. A blonde lock of hair tumbles to the ground and I watch in awe as it hits the marble floor. Bending down, I carefully pick it up and turn it over in my hands.

'More...' I whisper, letting it fall through my fingers. 'Much more.'

'But that's already twelve inches.' Aldo holds a mirror behind my head to show me the length. 'Any shorter and you won't be able to do much with it.'

'I don't care.' I tap my shoulders and smile up at him. 'Take it to here.'

Holding my gaze for a moment too long, he takes the scissors to my hair once more. My shoulders feel looser with every strand of hair that floats past my face. Each snip feels like a huge release as I relax my body and listen to the rhythmical sound of the blades crossing one another. Keeping my eyes fixed on the ground, I watch the blonde pile slowly grow into a mountain of cuttings.

I have always clung on to my blanket-like hair, convinced it shielded me from the rest of the world. If these past few months have taught me anything, it's that absolutely nothing can keep you safe from yourself. Once the monster inside hits that self-destruct button, no magic potion, no mythical mane of hair and no pills can save you, until you choose to save yourself.

Aldo runs his fingers through my hair before sectioning off the crown and fluffing up the rest. The snip of the scissors is like therapy and I allow myself to revel in the moment. When I finally open my eyes, I blink repeatedly to get my eyes to focus. Looking down at my chest, I smile as I realise I can no longer see my hair.

Reaching up to touch it, I yelp as Aldo bats away my hands. 'I'm not finished!' He growls, rummaging around in his work bag and producing various hair products.

After smoothing a selection of different serums through my now shoulder-length hair, he plugs in his trusty hairdryer and gets to work. The heat burns my neck slightly as Aldo picks up a brush and does what he does best. I sneak a peek at him and smile to myself as I watch him work. His face is taught with concentration as he manipulates my hair into the style he desires.

'Alright...' With a final spritz of hairspray, Aldo stands back to admire his handiwork. 'What do you think?'

Spinning around to face the mirror, I let out a squeal as I take in my reflection. I don't even recognise myself. How can something as simple as a haircut transform your entire appearance? The long bob makes my hair look thicker, healthier and shinier than it ever has before. My eyes seem brighter, my teeth seem whiter, even my skin looks better now it isn't hidden beneath the greying shadows of my hair.

'I love it.' I gush, shaking my head from side to side. 'I can't believe I didn't do it sooner. Thank you so much!'

Aldo leans down and sweeps my fringe across my forehead. Using his fingers, he expertly flips it from one side to the next before settling on the left and nodding appreciatively.

'You look good, Shirley...' He pulls me into a hug and plants a kiss on the top of my head. 'Really good.'

Beaming back at him, I stare at myself in the mirror and enjoy the rush of adrenaline. I can't believe how much volume I have now. How can cutting hair off possibly give you the illusion of having more? Too lost in my new reflection, I almost don't hear the authoritative knocking at the door.

'I'll get it.' Aldo sighs, giving my shoulder a squeeze as he steps over the pile of hair cuttings.

Knocking a few stray strands of hair from my shoulders, I unclip the cape and place it back into Aldo's work bag. I am about to sweep up the mess when I hear a commotion at the door and look up to see Piper, Ivy and Zara pushing their way inside.

Piper lets out a horrified gasp as her eyes land on the aftermath of my haircut. 'What have you done?'

'Do you like it?' I ask timidly, already sensing that she obviously does not.

'It's a little... Gone Girl.' Zara remarks, picking up a strand of my hair and letting it fall back down. 'You really *must* be losing it.' Letting out a bloodcurdling laugh, she scowls as she realises I don't find her joke funny. 'Oh, lighten up! I'm kidding!'

Humiliation hits me and I try to ignore it. Refusing to let panic back into my body, I grab a brush from behind the fridge and start to clear up the hair.

'How was your therapy?' Piper asks, shooting Zara a smirk. 'Still cray-cray?'

Cray-cray? Does she have any idea of the torment people with anxiety go through? Has she put an ounce of thought into the struggles they face on a daily basis?

'Actually, I'm glad you brought that up.' I pause with my brush on the pile of hair as my blood starts to boil. 'If any of you had bothered to give me the time of day, you would have realised I've been having a pretty hard time lately. Whatever image you have conjured up in your minds, double it and you're still not even close.' My voice becomes thunderous as fury rushes through my veins. 'Dealing with anxiety, depression and panic attacks has left me lower than any of you can imagine.

I've felt empty, frightened and more alone than I ever thought possible. So, if that makes me *cray-cray*, Piper, then that is *exactly* what I am!'

Three vacant faces stare blankly back at me and I suddenly have a surge of anger. I don't know whether it's the new hair or my chat with Ruby yesterday, but something inside me just snaps.

'You know it isn't contagious, don't you?' Folding my arms, I take a step towards Piper and she immediately recoils. 'It's not like having a cold or gastroenteritis. You can't catch it from shaking hands or kissing. Do you even know anything about mental illness? Anxiety? Depression?'

'Why are you being weird?' Zara asks, giving me a cautious glance. 'I think you need to see a doctor...'

'Already done that.' I fire back, resting my hands on my hips. 'You know, hence the anxiety and depression diagnosis.'

Just like the last time we bumped into one another, Ivy says nothing and plays with the collar of Spencer's jacket nervously. Guilt washes over her face as she realises I'm staring at her.

'Ivy, I know...' Keeping my eyes fixed firmly on hers, I almost feel sorry for her as she looks back at me like a lost child. 'I know and I honestly don't care.' I add, before she has the chance to interject. 'I will say I'm surprised. If it had to be one of you, I would have put my money on Piper.'

Piper starts to defend herself and I silence her by raising my hand.

'Spencer will do the same to you as he did to me. The fact that he cheated *with* you should be the first indicator that he will cheat *on* you.' I run my eyes over the jacket and then look down at my finger tattoo. 'I'm sure you would love the chance to explain *how* and *why* it happened. To try and convince me that you can't help who you fall in love with, but please believe me when I say, I really don't care. All I care about right now is getting back to a healthy state of mind.'

I take a step back and look at the other two, who are whispering to one another by the kitchen island. 'Don't worry, I'm very aware that support groups, counselling and alternative therapies aren't really on your agenda, so I don't expect you to stick around for the ride. Go back to your cocktails, manicures and meaningless conversations about men and money. Don't let me keep you.'

Stomping across the tiles, I throw open the door and signal for them to leave. 'Go on, what are you waiting for?'

Not bothering to dignify me with a response, they turn on their stilettoes and skulk out into the lobby, heads bowed and tails between their legs like a pack of guilty hyenas. Slamming the door shut behind them, I finally allow myself to breathe.

'Did that just happen?' I gasp, steadying myself on the wall as Aldo races across the room and plucks me up like a tiny child.

'It certainly did, Shirley!'

His eyes sparkle as he spins me around in the living room. 'And let me tell you something, if you can beat those three as easily as that, you've got this anxiety business in the bag...'

Chapter 24

Smiling at the nail technician, I watch the tiny fish nibbling at my toes and wonder if they're aware that I'm on the verge of a panic attack. With Aldo having a busy day at the salon, I agreed to come along for a pampering session. Despite the lingering sense of dread inside me, I'm desperately trying to look like I'm having a good time. At first, I felt great, but as the hours slip by my mind keeps drifting back to the stack of letters that are stuffed at the bottom of my handbag.

When the mail arrived this morning, I expected nothing more than a couple of pizza menus and perhaps the odd bank statement. I certainly did *not* expect a bunch of angry, red envelopes bearing demands for money. I must confess that I haven't been keeping track of my financial affairs lately. If I really think about it, I haven't so much as looked at my online banking in weeks, if not *months*. As far as I was concerned, the cheque from Precious was just sitting there. Surely the utility bills and household direct debits couldn't have burned through that much money so quickly?

I didn't let Aldo see the debt letters. He pays an agreed fee straight into my account each month, for all he knows everything is above board and up to date.

'Did you pick a colour?' The nail technician asks, pointing to the rows of neatly stacked bottles on the counter and drying my feet with a towel.

I scan the display and try to feel a connection with one of the pretty shades. Every colour of the rainbow winks back at me as I run my eyes over the impressive collection.

'This one.' I say decidedly, plucking a bottle from the shelf and silently remarking on how it matches the letters I received this morning.

My heart skips a beat as I wonder how I am going to stay in the black without an income. I've not been in the right state of mind to think about money, but now that it's been brought to my attention I can't think about anything else.

I catch a glimpse of Aldo and give him a quick wave. Wrestling with a head of brunette curls, he shoots me a concerned frown and I quickly fix my face into a smile. Tearing my eyes away, I nod approvingly at my red toenails and try to stop my ears from ringing. The worst thing about this anxiety is that it comes and goes like the wind. Just when I think I am turning a corner, it returns with a vengeance and gives me a blow to the stomach. One step forward and two steps back.

'Not today, Ann.' I whisper to myself, closing my eyes and silently counting to ten. 'Not today...'

'Who's Ann?' The nail technician giggles and reaches for a glossy top coat.

'Oh, I was just talking to my anxiety...' I stammer, laughing nervously. 'Giving it a name helps me to reason with it.'

'That's a great idea!' She remarks, tossing her French braid over her shoulder. 'I should do that with mine.'

'Do you have anxiety too?' My eyes widen as I wait for her to answer.

'I do.' She confirms, grabbing a bottle of cuticle oil. 'Not majorly, but with health-related issues.'

'What do you mean?' Taking a sip of the water she gave me earlier, I find myself starting to relax again.

'For example, if I get a headache, I'll convince myself I have a brain tumour.' She rolls her eyes and organises the products she's been using. 'People think it's funny, but I make myself physically sick. Just last month I had a bad dose of the flu and I was adamant I had some form of cancer. I was constantly visiting my doctor, demanding various tests to rule out anything sinister. My mum calls me a hypochondriac, but it's more than that. I work myself up to the point I'm having panic attacks and don't want to leave the house.'

'I'm sorry to hear that. I have panic attacks too, so I know how awful they are...' I offer her an understanding smile and wait for her to continue talking.

'Looking back at my meltdowns, I actually laugh at myself for overreacting, but I know I will be exactly the same the next time I feel ill.' She dips a cotton bud into the nail polish remover and tidies up my pedicure. 'When I slip into that bubble, I can't accept the previous occasions where I behaved so erratically.'

'I can completely relate to that. Anxiety can have frightening effects on the body and mind.' I purse my lips and watch her apply the finishing touches to my toes. 'Have you ever tried counselling?'

'I think I'm beyond counselling.' Spraying a dry oil onto my nails, she pumps moisturiser into her hands and covers the tops of my feet. 'Counselling is for people with real problems, isn't it?'

'Counselling can help all forms of anxiety. If it's affecting your quality of life, you should address it.' Reaching into my handbag, I produce a card from Anxiety Anonymous and pass it to her. 'This is a local support group, they hold meetings just around the corner. Give it a try, I think it might surprise you.'

Taking the card, she wipes her hands on a towel and slips it into her top pocket. 'Thank you so much. The next time I have an episode, I might just pay them a visit...'

I smile back at her as she excuses herself to see to another customer. Watching her talk animatedly to a tanned lady at the till, I find myself thinking about the many different forms anxiety can take. I'm shocked by how many triggers there are and just how many people are truly affected. My dealings with anxiety and depression are hopefully short-lived, but for some people, it controls their every movement, their inner happiness and their life choices.

I lean down to zip up my handbag and my fingers land on the letters I crammed in there earlier, resulting in my body immediately tensing up. Whilst I was listening to the nail technician talk, I didn't think about my own anxiety once. Casting my mind back to my meeting with Ruby, I recall one of the many pieces of advice she gave me.

Distraction is your secret weapon. If it's not worth your time, keep it off your mind.

Grabbing my phone, I bring up the forum to see if anyone else has commented on how effective this technique is. I am waiting for the page to load when the mobile rings in my hand. It's my mother. Taking in the name on the screen, I try to work out how I feel. Happy that she has finally called? Annoyed that it has taken her so long? I hover over the *accept* button before deciding to hit *reject*. Her name disappears into blackness and I breathe a sigh of relief. Talking to her isn't going to help me right now. I need to surround myself with people who lift me up, people who will be there when I need them and have my best interests at heart.

Julia speaks a lot about the importance of detaching ourselves from the negative influences around us. After all, a sinking ship has more chance of staying afloat if you throw out the things that are weighing it down...

Chapter 25

Taking a seat at the circle, I scan the room and wonder if any of these people are on the forum. The many hours I've spent scouring the threads have resulted in me becoming acquainted with quite a few users. I know their thoughts and their deepest, darkest feelings, but I have no idea of their real names. It's like I have seen their alter egos, the side of them no one else knows exist.

The chairs slowly fill up and I notice Ruby making her way down the lobby. Raising my hand, I tap the seat beside me and move my chair over.

'Your hair looks amazing!' She beams, dropping down onto the chair and shaking off her coat. 'You look so different! I almost didn't recognise you!'

'Thank you!' I reply, fluffing up my hair and smiling.

'What made you go for the chop?' Twisting her own hair into a ponytail, she waves at a few other members of the group.

'I don't really know. I've always been quite protective of my hair, but I felt like the time was right to let it go. My best friend is a hairdresser and he's been wanting to get his hands on it for years.'

'That's great!' She grins back at me and smooths down her tartan dress. 'I take it you're feeling better then?'

'I am. I had a little wobble yesterday, but the forum and the apps have really helped me.' I lower my voice as Julia steps into the room. 'How have you been?'

'Did you have a wobble?' Julia interjects before Ruby can answer and I feel the blood drain from my face. 'Do you want to share your experience with the group?'

The rest of the people in the room turn to stare at me and I suddenly feel incredibly light-headed. 'It was nothing, really...'

Julia ignores my dismissal and smiles broadly. 'I don't think we have been properly introduced. What's your name?'

I clear my throat and try to stop my cheeks from flushing violently. 'It's Sadie.'

'And what caused your wobble, Sadie?' Julia pushes her glasses into her hair and looks at me eagerly. 'What's your trigger?'

Not wanting to look anyone in the eye, I fidget with the hem of my shirt. 'I don't think I have just one trigger. I've been feeling really low and having panic attacks on and off for a while now. I thought I was making progress, but yesterday I was confronted with a problem and I felt all the usual symptoms coming back to me…'

'And what was this problem?' Julia holds her hands in her lap and stares at me with an unreadable expression on her face. 'It's fine if you would rather not say, but I can assure you this is a safe space. Absolutely everything you say here is confined to these four walls.'

Ruby twists a huge opal ring around her middle finger and motions for me to speak up.

'It was a financial problem. I have let things go these past few months and I've got myself into a bit of a pickle.' I dare to look up and find people nodding along.

A man in a suit clears his throat and leans forward in his seat. 'I can totally relate to that. Providing for my wife and three kids is what I live for. Just thinking about finances gives me anxiety. I think we can all agree that money is a common trigger.'

The rest of the group mumble in agreement and I breathe a sigh of relief.

'Have you always been a sufferer?' He asks, taking a sip from his paper cup. 'I noticed you at the last meeting too.'

'Actually, this is all new to me. It started with a breakup. One thing led to another and I found myself at rock bottom, but I'm glad to say I'm starting to feel better. Hopefully, I will be able to pull myself out of this hole as quickly as I fell into it.'

'That is very possible, Sadie.' Julia's calming voice causes the rest of us to turn her way. 'Matters of the mind are very subjective. Some people are affected for very short periods of their lives and others struggle for years on end. That is not to say the people who aren't affected for prolonged periods of time are going through any less hardship than long-term sufferers.' She pauses and fixes her gaze directly on me. 'I have a theory that experiencing anxiety first-hand can help us to become stronger mentally. Just like the old saying, *what doesn't kill us makes us stronger*.'

I let her words sink in as another member of the group speaks up about her own experience.

'Yesterday was the first day in an entire year that I braved the supermarket.' A mature, blonde lady declares proudly. 'For twelve months, I just haven't been able to face it. The people, the car park, the noises… Ordering online from the safety of my living room had become the norm for me, but yesterday I had this fresh surge of determination and told myself, *today is the day I take my life back*.' A round of applause erupts as she blinks back tears.

'That's fantastic, Rhian!' Julia beams brightly and hands her a box of tissues. 'Good for you!'

'I was just sat there in my dressing gown, adding carrots to my digital basket and I thought *no!* Enough is enough.' Her eyes glass over as she speaks. 'I can't pretend I wasn't afraid. I was shaking like a leaf as I made the short drive across town, but just knowing that I came face-to-face with anxiety and kicked its arse has given me so much confidence. If I can do it once, I can do it again.'

'You *can* do it!' Julia says encouragingly. 'You can *all* do it. Just like Rhian, you are all stronger than you seem and smarter than you believe. If you aren't quite there yet, don't panic, don't kick yourself and don't compare your journey with that of others.'

Just like the last time I was here, I feel a warmth wrap around me as I listen to Julia's words of wisdom. Being here makes me feel close to the old me, it gives me hope that I can and I *will* beat this.

'Like Sadie, don't be discouraged if you seem to be on the path to wellness and hit a stumbling block. In life, things will always test our strengths and our weaknesses. Do not crumble if you feel those old symptoms coming back to haunt you. It's completely normal to experience anxiety in certain situations.' Julia's voice sends me into a slightly hypnotic state as I soak up her words like a sponge.

'Money troubles, marital problems and family affairs are all examples of occasions where anxiety is totally normal. With the techniques you have learned in this group, you should be able to manage your anxiety before it spirals out of control and if you don't succeed in reigning it in from time to time, that's also okay. The one thing to remember with anxiety is, you will never know how strong you truly are until being strong is the only choice you have...'

Following Julia down the hallway, I haul my handbag onto my shoulder and tap her on the back. 'Do you have a moment?'

She stops with her hand on the door and spins around. 'Is everything okay, Sadie?'

'Yes, everything's fine...' I lick my dry lips and step to the side to allow the other members of the group to leave. 'I just wanted to thank you.'

Julia zips up her coat and pulls a khaki scarf out of her handbag. 'What on earth for?'

'I can't stress enough how much Anxiety Anonymous has helped me over the past few weeks. I don't know what I would have done if I wouldn't have found your group.'

'Well, I'm delighted you have found the support here beneficial, but there's absolutely no need to thank me. Helping people through the hard times is exactly what I'm paid to do. It's my job.' Julia pulls open the door to the street and I blink repeatedly for my eyes to adjust to the sunlight. 'What do you do for work, Sadie?'

'I'm an artist or at least I *was* an artist...'

'An artist!' She repeats, falling into step next to me. 'What kind of art?'

'I do paintings, mainly abstract. Precious used to display my pieces, but they can no longer accommodate me...'

'That's a shame. I'm sorry to hear that.' Julia swaps her glasses for shades as we weave through the crowds of people. 'What will you do now?'

I shrug my shoulders and exhale loudly. 'To be completely honest, I don't have a clue. I'll always paint, even if it's just for a hobby, but I think it's time to find a job with a steady income. I mean, I'm not getting any younger.'

Julia nods and seems deep in thought as we cross the street. 'What qualifications do you have?'

'I have a Sociology degree, not that I've ever used it. I'm ashamed to admit I fooled around through university, but even after years of tequila shots and wild nights out, I managed to scrape a 2:1. Miraculous, I know...' I give her a sideways glance and I'm relieved to see she is smiling.

'I haven't really put much thought into what I will do next, although from a financial stand point I need to work it out pretty quickly. Coming to the meetings has made me think about choosing a career in helping other people, like you do. Although I probably wouldn't be any good at it and I am guessing that you need a ton of qualifications...'

'Not necessarily and a Sociology degree is a fantastic place to start.' Julia's earrings jangle together as we head towards the car park.

'Have you always been a counsellor?' I ask, as she digs a set of keys out of her pocket and unlocks a red estate car.

Opening the boot, she tosses in her belongings and bites her lip as she thinks. 'This is my tenth year, but before that I worked in banking.'

'Wow!' I exclaim. 'That's a big change.'

'It is.' She agrees, taking off her coat and folding it neatly. 'I got into the world of banking at a very young age. I committed my entire life to it. I gave up the chance of a husband, children and a family to call my own, all for the money. I had been in the job for twenty years when my mother died suddenly and I was left completely alone. It was a huge wake-up call for me. I went through a *very* dark time, just like all of you at the meetings. When I finally pulled myself together, I decided to spend whatever time I had left on this planet helping others to overcome the same things I went through.'

I feel frozen to the spot, completely in shock to learn someone as calm and collected as Julia could have been a sufferer as well.

'The second I sent off the application I just knew it was the right decision for me. There's absolutely no better feeling than helping others.' Julia's eyes twinkle as she speaks, her passion for her job beaming out of her. 'It's like Christmas morning every single day. Watching people open the gift of wellness is something that money just can't buy. Although it's not all cupcakes and rainbows, in this role you have to share parts of yourself that you would normally keep sacred. I think the one question you have to ask yourself when becoming a counsellor is, are you willing to make that sacrifice?'

My mind goes into overdrive as I ask myself that same question. Could I really open myself up like that? Let's face it, not talking about my feelings is how I ended up here in the first place.

Jumping into the driver's seat, Julia buckles her seatbelt and starts up the engine. 'It's been lovely talking to you, Sadie. I'll see you at the next meeting.'

'Most definitely.' I give her a wave and step back as she puts the car into gear.

Watching her drive away, I slowly make my way over to my own car and replay our conversation in my mind. I can't believe

Julia was a banker, I really can't. I try to envisage her in a slick suit, barking orders into a headset whilst she looks at the FTSE 100. She's just so calming, so timid and gentle. It's almost laughable.

'Sadie?' A voice pops my thought bubble and I look around to see Patrick striding towards me.

'Wow! I am *loving* this new look!' Juggling a tray of coffee cups, he holds out his cheek for an air kiss. 'You look fabulous!'

'Thank you!' I automatically touch my hair and smile back at him. 'I guess I fancied a change...'

'Well, it certainly gets the thumbs-up from me.' Resting the tray of drinks on the bonnet of my car, he holds me at arm's length and gives me a quick once-over. 'Marvellous! I'm so pleased you're feeling better. I really, *really* am!'

'Thank you.' I look down at the ground awkwardly and decide to change the subject. 'How are things with Precious? Is the refurbishment coming along well?'

Patrick rolls his eyes and groans dramatically. 'I hate to say it, but it has been an absolute nightmare. Kieran and I have *very* different ideas on interior design. It's been a testing time, to say the least.'

Knowing very well just how much hard work Kieran can be, I give him a sympathetic smile and kick up a pile of leaves.

'Have you found a new venue for your work?' He asks, discreetly stealing a glance at his watch.

My heart skips a beat as I recall my conversation with Julia. 'Actually, I am thinking of a change in career...'

'A change in career?' Patrick cries in disbelief. 'You were born to be an artist! This isn't because of Precious, is it?'

'Oh, no!' I shake my head vehemently. 'It's not that. I just feel like I need to take my life in a different direction.'

Patrick studies my face for a moment before breaking into a smile. 'Well, good for you, Sadie. I'm sure you're making the right decision. After all, who knows what's better for you, than you?'

'Exactly!' I twirl my keys around my finger and press the key fob.

Taking this as his cue to leave, Patrick pulls me into a hug before picking up his coffees. 'I better let you go. I'm so glad our paths crossed. Don't be a stranger, okay?'

Nodding in response, I promise to call him and dive into the car. The radio automatically springs into action as I turn over the engine and set off back home. For the ten minutes it takes me to arrive back at the apartment and jump into the lift, I try and fail to imagine myself in a different role. Art is the only thing I've ever been any good at. Well, that and drinking champagne, but I don't think that is going to get me a well-paid job anytime soon.

Letting myself in, I grin happily as I spot Aldo and Edward's matching brogues sitting neatly on the shoe rack.

'How was the meeting?' Aldo yells from the living room.

Kicking off my ankle boots, I wander through the kitchen and find him sprawled out on the couch. 'It was great! Where's Edward?'

Aldo points to the bathroom and offers me his bag of crisps. Despite my attempts to stay positive, I haven't had the best appetite lately and I look at the packet sceptically. Remembering Ruby's words, I stick two fingers up to Ann and dive into the bag.

Reaching into his pocket, Aldo holds up a key and drops it onto the coffee table. 'That's the spare key to your mum's house. I sent someone over to fix the bathroom door.'

Shame washes over me as the memories of that night come racing back to me like a bad dream.

'You didn't have to do that...' I whisper, silently praying that Edward can't overhear our conversation. 'But thank you.'

'It was nothing.' Aldo dismisses my appreciation and rolls onto his side. 'Whilst we are on the subject, have you heard from your mum?'

'Yes and no.' I reply, ignoring the dread I feel at the mention of my mother. 'She called the other day, but I didn't answer. I need to fix myself before I try and fix our relationship.'

Aldo nods in agreement and finishes off the crisps. 'You're doing so well. The difference in you after just a few weeks is incredible. I'm so proud of you, Shirley.'

I choose not to say anything for fear of getting emotional as Edward walks out of the bathroom.

'Look at you!' He beams, jumping onto the couch next to me. 'You're like a whole new woman!'

'Do you like it?' I ask, secretly loving all these compliments on my new hairdo.

'I *love* it! I can't believe this is the first time I'm seeing it!' Edward gushes, looking at his own hair in the mirror. 'Maybe *I* could do with a makeover? Do you think you could make me look as good as Sadie?'

'I'm good, but I'm not *that* good...' Aldo teases, causing Edward to throw himself at him playfully.

Watching the two of them laugh and giggle as they bat one another with cushions, I try to remember the last time I saw Aldo so happy. Joy shines out of him as he pleads with Edward to stop tickling him. What would I have done without my dear friend? Aldo Cristiano Taylor, my guardian angel. He saved my life. Without Aldo, I wouldn't be sat here right now. Suddenly knowing what I need to do, I take a deep breath and clear my throat to gain their attention.

Immediately falling into silence, the pair of them stop what they're doing and sit up straight.

'I want you to move in with Edward.' I say decidedly, fixing my gaze on Aldo. 'You have been a rock to me through his terrible time and I will never be able to thank you enough.' My bottom lip starts to tremble, and this time I am powerless to stop it. 'You held me when I cried, picked me up when I fell and refused to give up on me when everyone else did.' I look away as I realise he has tears in his eyes. 'I owe you more than words can say, but now is the time for you to move on. You have done more for me than any friend ever should, but now I need to let you go. I'm not out of the woods just yet, but I need to figure out this last part of my journey alone...'

The three of us sit in an emotional silence before Aldo finally relents.

'I love you.' He mouths, roughly wiping his eyes as he struggles to compose himself.

'I love you too...' Not taking my eyes off his, I exhale sharply and try not to erupt into floods of tears.

'And I love *both* of you guys!' Edward sniffles, reaching out and pulling me onto his lap.

Throwing my arms around the pair of them, I squeeze tightly and plant a kiss on each of their foreheads. I may have a mother who is more interested in Pina Coladas, an empty bank account and absolutely no idea what's going to happen next in my life, but I do have an incredible best friend and with good friends by your side, you can get through just about anything...

Chapter 27

Howling in hysterics, I clutch my sides and try to stop my stomach from throbbing. I can't remember the last time I had this much fun. My cheeks are aching from giggling and my belly feels like I've done a hard-core workout. Struggling to regain my composure, I gasp for breath and lean against a tree trunk.

'*Stop!*' I beg. 'I can't take it anymore...' I try to keep my voice stern, but Ruby carries on regardless.

'Then it started to roll towards the swimming pool!' Her faces creases with laughter as she recalls her most embarrassing moment. 'I could have died!'

Not being able to look at her, I turn to face the tree as Ruby giggles with humiliation. I needed this, even more so than the meetings. Laughter is something that has been missing from my life for so long. I had almost forgotten what it felt like to let yourself go like this.

'Your turn!' Ruby stops on a bench to tie her shoelaces and pulls a bottle of water out of her backpack. 'What's your most embarrassing moment?'

Shaking my head in response, I stretch out my hamstrings and continue on our walk. 'If I told you, I would have to kill you.'

'Oh, come on!' She begs, jumping to her feet and running after me. 'I told you mine!'

'Let's just say it involved gin, Waitrose and Aldo...' My toes curl as I remember that mortifying day.

Ruby chuckles as she tries to fathom what chaos could have possibly ensued in the aisles of our local supermarket.

Giving her a playful nudge as we make our way through the bare trees, I pause to take a picture of the clear sky. 'I told you all you needed was some fresh air...'

'You were right.' She agrees, jumping over a muddy puddle. 'We lost Frank a while back.'

Feeling rather pleased with myself that I've succeeded in my mission, I give myself a mental pat on the back and march on ahead. When I was scouring through the Anxiety Anonymous forum this morning, I was saddened to see Ruby had posted numerous messages about a series of panic attacks. Reading her pleas for advice really struck a chord with me and I decided to take the plunge and invite her to meet up.

'Here we are...' We come to a stop by the huge rock and I point to the view below. 'Isn't it beautiful?'

Ruby drops her backpack and shields her eyes from the sun. 'Wow! I can't believe I've never been up here before!'

Clambering to the very tip of the rock, she pulls her phone out of her jacket and crouches down to take some photos. Luckily, the sun broke through the clouds a few minutes ago and is casting the incredible view of Cheshire in an illuminating light. I tip back my head and breathe deeply, trying to commit this feeling to memory.

Ruby rambles about how stunning the view is and I nod along, feeling guilty about the last time I was up here. I just couldn't appreciate it. I couldn't bring myself to appreciate *anything*. I was so empty, so void of any emotion that wasn't negative. I've come so very far in such a short space of time. Now I see hope. I see possibilities. I see a whole world out there that is just waiting for me to reach out and take it.

I sneak a peek at Ruby and remark at how strong she is to have carried Frank with her for so long. At first, I thought I was so unlucky to have been struck with anxiety, but now I'm thanking my lucky stars that my dealings with Ann seem to be short-lived. I'm one of the few who are fortunate enough to have kicked it to the curb before things got really nasty.

'I can see why you love this place.' Ruby beams, finally putting her phone away and sitting cross-legged on the rock. 'It's breath-taking.'

'I knew you would like it.' I drop down next to her and sigh. 'This is where I come when I want to escape reality for a little while. It's always been special to me, maybe it can be your special place, too?' Ruby looks out over the impressive landscape and nods. 'Whenever you feel like things are getting too much, or Frank decides to pay you a visit, just pop on your trainers and bring yourself up here.'

'Does coming here stop your anxiety every time?' Offering me her water bottle, she pulls a towel from her backpack and wipes her forehead.

'Not all the time, but just because I couldn't see the woods for the trees, doesn't mean that you won't.' I spot a smear of mud on my hand and use Ruby's towel to clean it off.

'Is that a tattoo?' Squinting closely, she cocks her head to one side to read the text. '*Forever*. What does it mean?'

I look down at my finger and find myself smiling. 'It doesn't mean anything. It's just a tattoo. Nothing more, nothing less.'

For the first time, I can answer that question and be truthful with my response. It genuinely doesn't mean anything to me anymore. I don't feel sad when I look at it. I don't have a rush of emotion when I think about the day It was etched onto my skin. I just see it for what it is, a beautiful inking.

'I've always wanted a tattoo.' Ruby muses, dangling her legs over the edge of the rock. 'My parents would go crazy though. They tell me that everyone with a tattoo regrets it eventually.' She rolls her eyes and tosses a pebble down the hill. 'Do you regret yours?'

'No.' I say decidedly. 'I went through a period where I did, but not anymore. If these past couple of months have taught me anything, it's that life's too short for regrets. We can't change the past, so we have to accept that at one time, things like tattoos were exactly what we wanted.'

Ruby takes my hand and inspects the tattoo more closely. 'I wish my parents were as cool as you.'

'I'm not cool.' I scoff, wrapping my arms around my knees. 'I had a nervous breakdown because of a failed relationship. I'm a loser...'

'That's not true. You went through a bad time and pulled yourself out of it. You rock.'

I feel my cheeks flush at her complimentary opinion of me. 'Thank you...'

'I should be the one thanking you. Today has been great. I feel so much better now.' She pushes herself up and offers me her hand. 'We should make this a regular thing, you know, like a buddy system. When Frank shows up, you call me and vice versa.'

I open my mouth to reply, but Ruby continues to babble.

'I don't mean all the time, obviously. I won't bother you in the middle of the night or anything.' Her face falls and she laughs nervously. 'Sorry, forget I said anything. You've probably got better things to be doing than dealing with my problems...'

I remember my conversation with Julia regarding helping others through the hard times and break into a smile. 'I think a buddy system sounds like a fabulous idea...'

'Really?' Ruby repeats cynically, stopping in her tracks.

'Really!' I confirm, linking my arm through hers. 'Removing Frank from your life is paramount and together we double our chances of beating him. Together we are stronger.' She gives me a thankful look and I respond with a wink. 'Just think, when *I* is replaced with *we*, even *illness* becomes *wellness*...'

* * *

Hitting *submit*, I double-check the listing and add the shoes to the overflowing pile on my left. A sense of accomplishment buzzes inside me as I scan the room for anything else that I no longer need. In a rather bold move, I decided that today would be the day I tackled my financial situation head-on. After a few rather uncomfortable phone calls to various banks and utility providers, I arranged a series of payment plans to get myself back on track. Without an income, I don't have any means of paying them, but in the meantime, I decided to have a clear out and try to generate some cash.

From expensive dresses to heaps of jewellery and a stack of signed records, everything I haven't used in the past year has been listed for sale online. I didn't intend on getting so carried away, but the more I looked for things, the more things I found and two hours later my bedroom is looking rather bare.

My phone pings on the dressing table and I'm delighted to discover more bids on my listings. Each time I hear that beep, I can literally see my debts reducing as people bid on my unwanted items. I wander over to my wardrobe and run my fingers over the remaining garments. Half a dozen pairs of jeans, a handful of jumpers and a selection of plain t-shirts now hang in the open space. Why did I ever think I needed those materialistic things? The shoes that made my feet rub, the dresses that pinched under the arms and the jewellery that was so eye-wateringly expensive I didn't dare wear. I picture them moving on to new beginnings, to new lives where they will be treasured and adored. Just like me, they will start a new chapter and leave this one behind.

I look at the mountain of clothes I didn't deem fit for sale and an idea suddenly hits me. Wandering into the kitchen, I rummage through the drawers for some bin liners and tear off a few bags. Grabbing handfuls of clothes, I fill three bags and head off in search of my car keys. With Aldo back at Edward's place, the apartment is back to being super quiet. Only this time it doesn't feel empty and intimidating. It feels open and peaceful in a way that it never has before.

When I waved goodbye to him, I was slightly concerned the panic attacks would return, but almost unbelievably I slept straight through the night. Not once did I stare up at the ceiling with my stomach churning. The moment my head hit the pillow my eyes naturally closed. The only thing causing my stomach to flutter was excitement of what my future will hold. Que sera sera, that is what I told myself as I drifted off and it's what I will keep telling myself every single day.

Light speckles shower down on me as I load up the car and set off on the short journey. I would normally walk, but the three bags I have in the boot weigh more than I do. The windscreen wipers go into overdrive as the rain becomes heavier, making it difficult to see as I race down the lane. Coming to a stop at a set of traffic lights, I prop my elbow on the arm rest as a flurry of school children cross the street. One by one they fall into line behind their teachers, each one wearing a high-visibility jacket as they run for cover from the rain.

Smiling to myself as I watch them splash around in the puddles, I release the handbrake and get set for the lights to change. I'm about to put my foot on the accelerator when my heart skips a beat. Turning up the wiper speed to clear the windows, I blink twice to make sure I'm not hallucinating. His stubble has grown into a hipster-style beard and his skin is several shades darker than I remember it, but it's definitely him. After all this time and all the heartache, Spencer Carter is just a few meters away from me. I study him through the rain-soaked window and try to find some connection with the man I once loved, but I don't feel a thing. It's like I don't even know him. Of course, I know his face, but it's as though I can't really recall why or where from.

Pressing his phone to his ear, our eyes meet for half a second before he starts to talk into the handset. He doesn't recognise me, probably the hair, either that or he just doesn't want to acknowledge me. I wait for the sadness to hit, or the pain that tormented me for so long to return, but it doesn't. I don't feel anything. The only emotion running through me is happiness, joy at finally being given confirmation that I am over Spencer Carter.

A car beeps behind me and I realise the lights have changed to green. Quickly putting the car into gear, I give him a final glance before slowly pulling away. For so long I have dreamt of this moment. The moment when our paths would cross again. I imagined all the horrible things I would say to him. The things I would do to make him experience the same pain he put me through, but now the time has come, all that anger has ebbed away. It's as though he's a villain from an old movie, one where I can't really remember the storyline, but I just know he's a bad guy.

Concentrating on the road ahead, I resist the urge to look in the rear-view mirror and turn up the radio. Spencer might be part of my past, but he isn't part of my future. It wasn't *him* making me feel so horrendous, I realise that now, it was the anxiety. It was the fear inside me that made me crumble and fall, not a man who I spent six months of my life with.

Seeing him today has made me realise just how monumental this journey has been. It's taken me on a whirlwind rollercoaster ride and I can finally see the finishing line. I might not be at my final

destination just yet, but something inside
is telling me that the best is yet to come...

Chapter 28

'Thank you so much for inviting me.' Ruby whispers, picking up a canapé and dropping it onto her plastic plate. 'This place is so cool!'

'You're welcome!' I flash her a smile and dunk a breadstick into a mound of guacamole.

'Don't they make a gorgeous couple?' She sighs, watching Aldo and Edward entertain guests on the balcony. 'I didn't know he was...'

'Gay?' I interrupt, already knowing what she's going to say. 'Not many people do.'

'He has great hair...' Not taking her eyes off Aldo, Ruby leans against the wall and stares shamelessly. 'And his eyes are so *blue*. Does he wear contact lenses?'

Rolling my eyes, I look around the room and rock my shoulders in time to the music. This belated moving out party is one of the best ideas I've ever had. Unbeknown to Aldo, I managed to plan the entire thing with Edward in just a couple of days. His face when he walked into the apartment was priceless. After how much he has helped me, I thought the least I could do was to wave him off in style.

Watching our friends laugh and rejoice together, I have to admit we've done a brilliant job. Music plays on the entertainment system, streamers hang from the ceiling and the kitchen is filled with yummy food and tempting drinks.

'Are you going to get a new roommate?' Ruby asks, taking a sip from her wine glass. 'This place is huge just for one person.'

'I'm not sure yet...' I turn around and watch Aldo's colleagues dance around the kitchen island. 'I think being alone for a little while would do me good.'

'I love being alone. It's rare that I get a moment of peace with my brothers running around the place all the damn time.' She screws up her nose and frowns. 'I can't wait to get my own apartment.'

I pull a wine bottle from the cooler and top up our glasses. 'Where exactly do you live?' I ask, suddenly aware that she hasn't ever divulged much about her home life.

'Mobberley.' Ruby digs a compact mirror out of her handbag and checks her teeth for lipstick. 'My parents have a farm.'

'A farm!' I repeat, borrowing her mirror to give my own makeup a quick once-over. 'So, you're a farm hand?'

'Please! Do you really think I could work the farm with these?' She waggles her acrylic nails in the air as Aldo joins us at the buffet.

'Do you mind if I steal my favourite girl for a moment?' He asks, squeezing past Ruby and taking me by the hand.

Excusing myself, I grab my drink with my free hand and let him lead me into the bathroom. The music floats in behind us as he shuts the door and sits on the edge of the bath.

'This is it, Shirley!' Aldo pulls out his bobble and lets his hair fall around his shoulders. 'The end of an era!'

'Where you and I are concerned, it will *never* be the end!' I drop down to the floor and lean against the shower cubicle. 'Edward might be your main man, but don't forget that *I* was here first…'

He leans over and ruffles my hair before taking a deep slug of wine. 'How could I ever…'

We have had so many amazing times here, both good and bad. Some of the best moments of my life happened in this apartment and some of the worst. The bass from the entertainment system makes the floor vibrate gently beneath me as I think back over our time together. I can almost see a film reel of our friendship playing over and over in my mind.

'Nothing has to change.' Aldo whispers, taking a seat on the tiles next to me.

'*Everything* has to change...' I correct, resting my head on his shoulder. 'I need a fresh start. I need to work out what I really want out of life, because an unreliable career and a ridiculously large apartment isn't it.'

'You'll figure it out, Shirley. I have every faith in you.' Aldo stretches out his legs and exhales loudly. 'I've said it before, but I'm going to say it again... I am *so* proud of how you have managed to turn things around.'

I look up at him and a whole world of emotions wash over me. 'I will never forget what you did for me, Aldo. Thank you...'

There are a million more things I could say to him, but I don't want to taint his leaving party with wine-fuelled, emotional goodbyes on the floor of my en-suite. Aldo knows just how much he means to me. We're lucky enough to have the kind of friendship where a single look can you tell you more than an entire conversation ever could. Knowing there's nothing left for us to say, we clink glasses and finish our drinks in silence, but it's a silence that says everything...

* * *

'Properties like this don't stay on the market for very long. We have a whole portfolio of clients waiting for premises of this nature.' The estate agent stands back and looks up at the apartment block. 'I can guarantee you a very quick sale, regardless of asking price.'

Taking an information pack from him, I run my eyes over the details and hold out my hand. 'Thank you so much for your time. There are a few things I need to think about, but I will get back to you with a decision shortly.'

'No problem. I shall look forward to hearing from you.' With a final smile, the estate agent picks up his briefcase and leaves me alone in the foyer.

Folding the paperwork neatly, I take the stairs back to the apartment and grab my mobile from the coffee table. All night I toyed with the idea of putting this place on the market, but now I have confirmation of the price and selling potential, I am more sure than ever that it's what I want to do. A luxury apartment in the heart of Alderley Edge was once exactly what my heart desired, but now it just seems so fragile and hollow. I don't want to spend my future desperately trying to make ends meet. I don't *need* a place this big. What I need is an actual home, somewhere I can make my own and start afresh.

I should really tell my mum about my decision, she did buy this place for me. Not wanting another earache about how ungrateful I am, I decide to put it into a text message and press *send*. Looking around the four walls that I've called my home for so many years, I silently thank it for the memories and pull on my trainers. The support group starts in thirty minutes and if I set off walking now, I should just about make it in time. Julia spoke in the last meeting about the many benefits exercise can have on the mind and today I am putting her theory to the test.

I pop in my earphones and close the door behind me as I set off on my journey. A part of me feels like a phoney for still attending the meetings, but I'm afraid I will slip straight back into a depression if I give it up so soon. Julia keeps reminding me everyone's battle with anxiety is different, but something tells me it's not quite done with me just yet.

Pounding the pavement, I quicken my pace to a jog and surprise myself with how I've kept my fitness. My lungs burn as I push myself to my limit, not stopping until I am in front of the Anxiety Anonymous building. Sitting down on a bench, I wait for my breathing to return to normal and shove my iPod into my bag. Once confident my face is no longer glowing, I push myself up and make my way inside.

The dark lobby now feels so welcoming to me as I push open the door to the meeting and scan the room. I spot Ruby chatting to a few of the regular members by the window and head over to join them.

'Hey!' Tapping her on the shoulder, I smile as she turns around and embraces me warmly. 'Wow! It's busy today.' I observe, taking in the many new people milling around the room.

'I know...' She frowns at her watch and passes me a cup. 'I'm a little concerned about Julia, she should be here by now. It's not like her to be late.'

Looking up at the clock on the wall, I'm surprised to discover that the meeting should have started five minutes ago.

'Did Aldo tell you he's doing my hair next week?' Ruby smiles as we choose two seats towards the front of the room.

'He did mention something...' I smile as she shows me a photograph of a model with aubergine waves. 'That's a gorgeous colour!'

After discussing Ruby's upcoming makeover, we fall into silence as the other seats slowly fill up. I watch the minutes tick by until a woman sat opposite speaks up.

'It looks like she isn't going to show...' Picking up her briefcase, she takes her coat from the rack as the rest of the room nod in agreement.

One by one people stand up and start to head for the door, disappointment filling the air. All of these people have come here today for the same reason. They're struggling so much with their mental health that they've taken the colossal step to actually stand up and ask for help. Some of them probably won't return after this. They will cross counselling off their list forever...

'I could stand in.' The words are out of my mouth before I can stop them. 'Just this once.' I add, preparing for my lame offer to be rejected.

'That's a great idea!' Ruby gushes enthusiastically, looking at the others for their reactions. 'What do you guys think?'

A man in parka coat shakes his head and slips out of the room, but to my astonishment, everyone else retreats to their seats. My ears ring with adrenaline as Ruby gives me the nudge I need to walk over to the chair at the head of the circle. What am I playing at? Twenty faces stare back at me as I curse myself for opening my big mouth.

'Well, as you all know, I am *not* a counsellor, but due to unforeseen circumstances I am going to try and fill some rather big shoes...'

A small laugh echoes around the room, calming my nerves and giving me a confidence boost.

'I might not be qualified to be sat in this chair, but I am here for the exact same reason as the rest of you.' My mouth becomes dry as I take in the many pairs of eyes burning into me. 'Until a few months ago, mental health wasn't something I ever really thought about, but after a series of, let's say *unfortunate* events in my life, I slipped into a dark hole that seemed impossible to crawl out of.'

My stomach flips as I realise I'm sharing my life with a room of complete strangers. I think back to the other meetings and marvel at how much trust these people put into Julia. I can't expect them to open up to me if I'm keeping my own story secret. Taking a deep breath, I decide to throw caution to the wind and jump in at the deep end.

'A few months ago... I tried to take my own life.' The words seem to tumble out of my mouth, as though they never should have been in there in the first place. 'Looking back, I didn't want to kill myself. It was a cry for help, a desperation call.' I look up to see everyone in the room nodding, indicating they understand exactly what I'm talking about. 'For a short while, anxiety and depression totally consumed me. They seeped into my life and completely took over my mind and body. Thankfully, I seem to have taken back the control and I'm in the process of getting back to the person that I used to be.'

A round of applause erupts and my cheeks flush with embarrassment.

'Thanks...' I mumble, genuinely touched by their support. 'The point I am making is that this is all new to me, but that doesn't mean I don't know what you're going through.' Sitting on my hands to stop them from shaking, I exhale deeply and force myself to smile. 'So, does anyone have anything they would like to share with the group?'

I brace myself for a deafening silence, only my jaw drops as I see a flurry of hands raised. Smiling at the nearest person to me, I motion for her to speak.

'I thought I was making progress with my anxiety. I convinced myself the worst was behind me.' Cracking her knuckles nervously, she shakes her head and I notice she has tears in her eyes. 'I haven't had a panic attack or an anxiety breakdown for at least a month, but last weekend I woke up with an awful feeling. At first, I thought I was ill. I told myself I was coming down with something, but then the usual symptoms returned.' Her voice wobbles and I feel her pain. 'The racing heart, sweaty palms and hideous feeling of dread that refuses to leave no matter what I do...'

I let her words sink in and take my mind back to the anti-anxiety apps that helped me so much.

'The one thing that helped me the most was to educate myself on what exactly panic attacks are.' I pause to collect my thoughts, praying the information I am telling her is correct. 'As scary and overwhelming as the physical effects of anxiety can feel, they are caused by nothing more than the overproduction of adrenaline. When we deem a situation to be potentially dangerous, whether that be a burning building or an overdue bill you just can't afford, our brains instruct the release of adrenaline. Adrenaline is an important part of our defence system as it warns us of dangers, but when we have too much adrenaline racing through our bodies it causes the unpleasant symptoms you are describing.'

I turn my attention to the rest of the group and feel myself relax into the role. 'When I had my first panic attack, I genuinely thought I was going to die. I had never experienced anything quite like it. Since I have accepted anxiety can't do me any harm, they have become much easier to manage. If you learn to recognize the very first signs of anxiety, you can use various techniques to stop it in its tracks...'

A man in a camouflage jacket raises his hand and coughs. 'Which techniques have you found to be the most effective?'

'The brain can be a very powerful thing and learning to control the way I react to situations is something that I am still battling, but simple methods such as controlled breathing and calming audio apps have proved extremely successful with me.' I cross my legs and point to Ruby. 'Ruby taught me a saying that I chant over and over in my mind whenever anxiety strikes...'

'This too shall pass?' Ruby finishes for me, smiling proudly.

'Yes!' I nod and smile back at her. 'I find myself repeating those four little words whenever I feel *anything* I don't like. Constantly reminding myself that everything is temporary enables me to see things a little more clearly. I say those words to remind myself that I *can* and *will* get through it.'

'I guess I can relate to that...' The man in camouflage leans forward in his seat and appears deep in thought. 'You mean like, it's just a bad day and not a bad life?'

'Exactly!' Ruby exclaims enthusiastically. 'I can be in the middle of a complete meltdown, but if I take a step back and look at what I've already come through, I know I can get past it.'

I wait for the other members in the room to stop talking before I continue.

'We are all so much stronger than we allow ourselves to believe. Regardless of what life has thrown our way, we are all still sat here today. Yes, we might have a few battle scars, but what doesn't kill us makes us stronger.' I move my eyes from one person to the next, taking in every feature on their faces. 'I know that compared to what most of you are going through, my short battle with anxiety pales into insignificance, but if my experience can help just one of you even a little bit, it will make the whole experience completely worth it...'

Chapter 29

'That was incredible!' Ruby squeals, waiting for the final person to leave before throwing herself at me. 'You were born to do this!'

'I wouldn't go that far...' Dismissing her praise, I tug on my coat and stack the last of the chairs neatly with the others.

'I'm being serious!' Ruby trails behind me excitedly as we make our way outside. 'Did you hear all the compliments they were giving you? How do you feel?'

'I feel great!' We step out onto the street and I pull up my hood to shield my hair from the rain. 'It's so liberating to help people, not that I think I was any good at it...'

'Don't put yourself down like that!' Ruby hits me on the arm and frowns. 'We all thought you were fabulous! Even *Alec* gave you the thumbs-up!'

Feeling uncomfortable with her praise, I decide to change the subject. 'Anyway, what are your plans for the rest of the day?'

'Nothing much...' She tries and fails to put up her umbrella before diving under a shop canopy for shelter. 'Do you want to get some lunch somewhere? We could grab a pizza?'

My mind flits back to my meeting with the estate agent and I automatically reach into my pocket for his card. 'Thanks for the offer, but I should probably head straight home. I have a few things I need to deal with.'

A look of panic flashes across Ruby's face before she quickly covers it with a smile. 'Nothing to do with Ann, I hope?'

I shake my head and turn to look in a shop window. 'No, Ann hasn't paid me a visit in a little while, thankfully.'

Ruby reluctantly accepts this and shrugs her shoulders. 'Fine, if I can't tempt you with lunch then I better leave you to get on your way. See you at the next meeting?'

'Definitely...' After saying our goodbyes, I brace myself for a walk home in the rain as Ruby heads off in the opposite direction.

She gets to the end of the road before stopping in her tracks and turning to face me. 'You *are* good at this, Sadie. Just remember that...'

A smile plays on my lips as I give her a nod before starting the return journey to the apartment. Julia was totally right.

Nothing feels as good as helping other people. Just knowing you've aided someone through a dark period gives you such a rush. No wonder she loves her job so much.

Picking up my pace as the rain becomes heavier, I notice a *for sale* sign outside the cute cottages to my right. Shielding my eyes from the driving rain, I give them a closer look and try to imagine myself living there. With quaint thatched roofs and pretty chocolate-box gardens, they seem perfect for a single person like me. I picture myself cooking healthy meals, planting bulbs in the flower beds and decorating the place in the shabby chic design that I secretly adore.

I'm still creating this make-believe life for myself when I come to a stop at the gates to my apartment. Noticing a red car parked on the opposite side of the street, I squint at the windscreen as it follows me inside. Dashing into the building for shelter, I spin around as I hear my name being called from the car park. Trying to pinpoint the location of the voice, I let out a shocked gasp as I see Julia clambering out of the car.

'Julia!' I beckon her inside and take off my wet jacket. 'What are you doing here?'

'I wanted to talk to you.' Holding her handbag above her head, she sprints up the steps two at a time. 'I really hope you don't mind me just showing up at your home?'

'Not at all.' I reply in confusion, tucking my damp hair behind my ears. 'How did you know where I lived?'

Julia looks down at the ground guiltily and twirls a bracelet around her wrist. 'I must confess that I had a little help from Ruby. Don't worry, I don't make a habit of turning up at member's homes!'

We both laugh and I bite my lip nervously. 'Why weren't you at the meeting?'

'That's a very good question.' She replies, smoothing down her blouse. 'I don't suppose you have time for a coffee, do you?'

'Coffee sounds great...' Motioning to the stairs, my stomach churns as I try to think of something to say.

'This is a beautiful building.' She remarks, hitching up her dress and following me up the staircase. 'It really is stunning.'

I turn to look out of the giant windows and nod in agreement. 'I know. I'm going to miss it.'

'You're moving?' Stopping to take in her surroundings, Julia shakes her head in disbelief. 'Why on earth would you leave a place like this?'

Digging around in my pockets for my keys, I unlock the door and lead the way inside. 'I can no longer afford the maintenance of it.' I answer honestly. 'Plus, the capital from the sale will give me a good cushion to sit on until I figure out what to do next.'

Julia seems deep in thought for a moment before clearing her throat. 'Well, that actually leads me on nicely to why I am here.'

I look at her expectantly, but bizarrely she doesn't say a word until I place a steaming cup of coffee in front of her. Sliding onto a stool at the opposite end of the kitchen island, I blow into my mug and wait for her to speak.

'We had a conversation a while ago about counselling and I saw something in you that played on my mind all evening. Your desire to help people is a quality so many of us lack.' Julia studies my face for a moment before carrying on. 'I intentionally didn't attend the meeting today...'

I shoot her a questioning look and wait for her to elaborate. Clearly choosing her words carefully, Julia rubs her hands together and exhales slowly.

'I've been offered a promotion...'

'A promotion?' I repeat, inadvertently cutting her off mid-sentence. 'That's fantastic!'

'It is fantastic, but it does mean that my position at the Wilmslow branch is going to be vacant.' She props her elbows on the table and purses her lips. 'Now, tell me if I am way off the mark here, but I think *you* would be a great candidate for the role.'

Me? I open my mouth to speak before closing it again, completely lost for words.

'Being a counsellor isn't an easy career choice. It can be tiring, emotionally draining and bloody hard work, but it's also one of the most rewarding things that you can do with your life...' She pauses to gauge my reaction and sighs. 'I knew you would step up to the plate today. I was in the assessment office the whole time. You were amazing, just as I thought you would be.'

My heart pounds in my chest as I try to process what exactly she's saying. Did she… did she set me up?

'The charity want someone with flair, someone who understands what these people are going through and you simply cannot do that if you haven't experienced it for yourself. I'd like to clarify that the money isn't fabulous and it certainly wouldn't pay for a place like this. You would also have to travel to Hale, Knutsford and Prestbury. I am assuming you have your own transportation?'

Feeling completely thrown, I manage a nod as my mind goes into overdrive.

'You would need to go on some courses and you would be in unpaid training for the first couple of weeks, but I feel like this position was made for you, Sadie. I really do.'

Trying to think clearly, I hold my head in my hands as her words ring around my mind. *This position was made for you.* How have I ended up here? This is just so surreal. I feel a million miles away from the girl that I once was. I feel like I am walking in someone else's shoes, living some else's life. The question is, is this the life I want to live?

'I understand this must be a lot to take in, but the charity is eager to secure a candidate for the role as soon as possible.' Julia leans over the table and places her tanned hand on my arm. 'The last thing I want to do is pressure you into taking the role, but my gut is telling me this is the right thing for you.'

I turn to look out of the window as I try to clear my mind and really think about what is being offered here. The trees in the distance stand perfectly still, giving the illusion they're holding their breath as they wait for me to answer. Closing my eyes, I take myself back to the Anxiety Anonymous meeting and remember how amazing it felt to be sat in that seat, to offer a helping hand to those in need and to guide them on their journey back to wellness.

Maybe *this* is who I am. Maybe I was destined to meet Spencer and go through all of this to lead me to where I am right now. To be sat on this stool, to be offered this role and to be given the opportunity to use my life to help others.

I open my eyes to see a sudden gust of wind cause the trees to shake violently, seemingly telling me what I need to do. A smile plays on my lips as I cast a final look around the apartment before fixing my gaze on Julia.

'So, Sadie, what do you say?'

Epilogue

Looking around the room, I smile at the many faces staring back at me.

Some relieved they're not alone in their struggle, some saddened by my experience and others just ready to share their own stories.

'So, that's everything. The good, the bad and the downright ugly.' My skin prickles as I cross my legs and adjust the stack of paperwork on my lap. 'Being a counsellor, you may think that sharing my own story with mental health comes naturally to me, but I can assure you it doesn't. Revisiting that time in my life brings up emotions I would much rather forget and I am sure you will feel the same about sharing your own thoughts and feelings.'

A few of the attendees fidget uneasily in their seats and I flash them what I hope is a reassuring smile.

'As uncomfortable as it makes you feel, when it comes to your mental health, talking is your medicine. It's the number one thing you should be doing. Whenever you are frightened, scared or afraid, speak up. Say it loud and say it proud. Never suffer in silence, never keep it bottled up and *never* feel like you are alone.'

I run my thumb along my finger tattoo as I talk, making sure to lock eyes with each and every person.

'My aim in these meetings is to make talking a normal part of your daily routine. I want you to see these meetings as *your* place. I want you to step into this room safe in the knowledge that you can say anything at all and not be judged. You might not feel ready to speak up just yet and that's completely fine. Just choosing to join us today is a huge step on your path back to wellness.'

Ruby beams proudly at me from the far end of the circle and I smile back at her.

'My own journey with anxiety and depression has led me to where I am today. It has moulded the person that I am and completely changed the direction my life was going in. Without the support of Anxiety Anonymous, I think the outcome would have been very different indeed...'

Hearing the door squeak open, I look over my shoulder to see Julia slipping into the room. Flashing me the thumbs up sign, she takes a seat amongst the others.

'This charity has been at the forefront of my success in overcoming anxiety and now I want to help all of you to beat it, too. It's time to stop sweeping matters of the mind under the carpet and hoping they'll disappear. It's time to end the stigma around asking for help. It's time to *talk*...'

To be continued...

If you are struggling with anxiety, help is available to you.

Mind Infoline

0300 123 3393

Anxiety UK Infoline

08444 775 774

Anxiety United

www.anxietyunited.com

Follow Lacey London on Twitter

@thelaceylondon

Other books by Lacey London

The Clara Andrews Series

Meet Clara Andrews

Clara Meets the Parents

Meet Clara Morgan

Clara at Christmas

Meet Baby Morgan

Clara in the Caribbean

Clara in America

Clara in the Middle

Clara's Last Christmas

The Clara series is exclusive to Amazon.

Meet Clara Andrews
Book 1

Meet Clara Andrews... Your new best friend!

With a love of cocktails and wine, a fantastic job in the fashion industry and the world's greatest best friends, Clara Andrews thought she had it all.

That is until a chance meeting introduces her to Oliver, a devastatingly handsome American designer. Trying to keep the focus on her work, Clara finds her heart stolen by Michelin starred restaurants and luxury hotels.

As things got flirty, Clara reminds herself that inter-office relationships are against the rules, so when a sudden recollection of a work's night out leads her to a cheeky, charming and downright gorgeous barman, she decides to see where it goes.

Clara soon finds out that dating two men isn't as easy as it seems...

Will she be able to play the field without getting played herself?

Join Clara as she finds herself landing in and out of trouble, re-affirming friendships, discovering truths and uncovering secrets.

Clara Meets the Parents Book 2

Almost a year has passed since Clara found love in the arms of delectable American Oliver Morgan and things are starting to heat up.

The nights of tequila shots and bodycon dresses are now a distant memory, but a content Clara couldn't be happier about it.

It's not just Clara things have changed for. Marc is settling in to his new role as Baby Daddy and Lianna is lost in the arms of the hunky Dan once again.

When Oliver declares it time to meet the Texan in-laws, Clara is ecstatic and even more so when she discovers that the introduction will take place on the sandy beaches of Mexico!

Will Clara be able to win over Oliver's audacious mother?

What secrets will unfold when she finds an ally in the beautiful and captivating Erica?

Clara is going to need a little more than sun, sand and margaritas to get through this one...

Meet Clara Morgan
Book 3

When Clara, Lianna and Gina all find themselves engaged at the same time, it soon becomes clear that things are going to get a little crazy.

With Lianna and Gina busy planning their own impending nuptials, it's not long before Oliver enlists the help of Janie, his feisty Texan mother, to help Clara plan the wedding of her dreams.

However, it's not long before Clara realizes that Janie's vision of the perfect wedding day is more than a little different to her own.

Will Clara be able to cope with her shameless mother-in-law Janie?

What will happen when a groom gets cold feet?

And how will Clara handle a blast from the past who makes a reappearance in the most unexpected way possible?

Join Clara and the gang as three very different brides, plan three very different weddings.

With each one looking for the perfect fairy tale ending, who will get their happily ever after...

Clara at Christmas
Book 4

With snowflakes falling and fairy lights twinkling brightly, it can only mean one thing - Christmas will be very soon upon us.

With just twenty-five days to go until the big day, Clara finds herself dealing with more than just the usual festive stresses.

Plans to host the perfect Christmas Day for her American in-laws are ambushed by her BFF's clichéd meltdown at turning thirty.

With a best friend on the verge of a mid-life crisis, putting Christmas dinner on the table isn't the only thing Clara has got to worry about this year.

Taking on the role of Best Friend/Therapist,

Head Chef and Party Planner is much harder than Clara had anticipated.

With the clock ticking, can Clara pull things together - or will Christmas Day turn out to be the December disaster that she is so desperate to avoid?

Join Clara and the gang in this festive instalment and discover what life changing gifts are waiting for them under the tree this year...

Meet Baby Morgan
Book 5

It's fair to say that pregnancy hasn't been the joyous journey that Clara had anticipated. Extreme morning sickness, swollen ankles and crude cravings have plagued her for months and now that she has gone over her due date, she is desperate to get this baby out of her.

With a lovely new home in the leafy, affluent village of Spring Oak, Clara and Oliver are ready to start this new chapter in their lives. The cot has been bought, the nursery has been decorated and a name has been chosen. All that is missing, is the baby himself.

As Lianna is enjoying new found success with her interior design firm, Periwinkle, Clara turns to the women of the village for company. The once inseparable duo find themselves at different points in their lives and for the first time in their friendship, the cracks start to show.

Will motherhood turn out to be everything that Clara ever dreamed of?

Which naughty neighbour has a sizzling secret that she so desperately wants to keep hidden?

Laugh, smile and cry with Clara as she embarks on her journey to motherhood. A journey that has some unexpected bumps along the way. Bumps that she never expected...

Clara in the Caribbean Book 6

Almost a year has passed since Clara returned to the big smoke and she couldn't be happier to be back in her city.

With the perfect husband, her best friends for neighbours and a beautiful baby boy, Clara feels like every aspect of her life has finally fallen into place.

It's not just Clara who things are going well for. The Strokers have made the move back from the land down under and Lianna is on cloud nine – literally.

Not only has she been Jetting across the globe with her interior design firm, Periwinkle, she has also met the man of her dreams... again.

For the past twelve months Li has been having a long distance relationship with Vernon Clarke, a handsome man she met a year earlier on the beautiful island of Barbados.

After spending just seven short days together, Lianna decided that Vernon was the man for her and they have been Skype smooching ever since.

Due to Li's disastrous dating history, it's fair to say that Clara is more than a little dubious about Vernon being 'The One.' So, when her neighbours invite Clara to their villa in the Caribbean, she can't resist the chance of checking out the mysterious Vernon for herself.

Has Lianna finally found true love?

Will Vernon turn out to a knight in shining armour or just another fool in tin foil?

Grab a rum punch and join Clara and the gang as

they fly off to paradise in this sizzling summer read!

Clara in America
Book 7

With Clara struggling to find the perfect present for her baby boy's second birthday, she is pleasantly surprised when her crazy mother-in-law, Janie, sends them tickets to Orlando.

After a horrendous flight, a mix-up at the airport and a let-down with the weather, Clara begins to question her decision to fly out to America.

Despite the initial setbacks, the excitement of Orlando gets a hold of them and the Morgans start to enjoy the fabulous Sunshine State.

Too busy having fun in the Florida sun, Clara tries to ignore the nagging feeling that something isn't quite right.

Does Janie's impromptu act of kindness have a hidden agenda?

Just as things start to look up, Janie drops a bombshell that none of them saw coming.

Can Clara stop Janie from making a huge mistake, or has Oliver's audacious mother finally gone too far?

Join Clara as she gets swept up in a world of fast food, sunshine and roller-coasters.

With Janie refusing to play by the rules, it looks like the Morgans are in for a bumpy ride...

Clara in the Middle
Book 8

It's been six months since Clara's crazy mother-in-law took up residence in the Morgan's spare bedroom and things are starting to get strained.

Between bringing booty calls back to the apartment and teaching Noah curse words, Janie's outrageous behaviour has become worse than ever.

When she agreed to this temporary arrangement, Clara knew it was only a matter of time before there were fireworks. But with Oliver seemingly oblivious to Janie's shocking actions, Clara feels like she has nowhere to turn.

Thankfully for Clara, she has a fluffy new puppy

and a job at her friend's lavish florist to take her mind off the problems at home.

Throwing herself into her work, Clara finds herself feeling extremely grateful for her great circle of friends, but when one of them puts her in an incredibly awkward situation she starts to feel more alone than ever.

Will Janie's risky behaviour finally push a wedge between Clara and Oliver?

How will Clara handle things when Eve asks her for the biggest favour you could ever ask?

WIth Clara feeling like she is stuck in the middle of so many sticky situations, will she be able to keep everybody happy?

Join Clara and the gang as they tackle more family dramas, laugh until they cry and test their friendships to the absolute limit.

Clara's Last Christmas
Book 9

The series has taken us on a journey through the minefields of dating, wedding day nerves, motherhood, Barbados, America and beyond, but it is now time to say goodbye.

Suave. It's where it all began for Clara and the gang and in a strange twist of fate, it's also where it all ends...

Just a few months ago, life seemed pretty rosy indeed. With Lianna back in London for good, Clara had been enjoying every second with her best friend.

From blinged-up baby shopping with Eve to wedding planning with a delirious Dawn, Clara and her friends were happier than ever.

Unfortunately, their happiness is short lived, as just weeks before Christmas, Oliver and Marc discover that their jobs are in jeopardy.

With Clara helping Eve to prepare for not one, but two new arrivals, news that Suave is going into administration rocks her to the core.

It may be December, but the prospect of being jobless at Christmas means that not everyone is feeling festive. Do they give up on Suave and move on, or can the gang work as one to rescue the company that brought them all together?

Can Clara and her friends save Suave in time for Christmas?

Join the gang for one final ride in this LAST EVER instalment in the series!